Adam,

I found this when I was gathering things for your dad to have after I die. But then I thought that someday it may be of value to you. So I'm saving it for you. I've even added some notes to you.

This started out as just another one of my many sketch pads but later turned into sort of a diary.

This is my story. But it's also your story because I'm a part of who you are. I am your birth mom. I love you. I will always love you.

JUNE 9

Dad called last night to tell me he'd be tied up all day at work and Mom couldn't get away either so he'd be sending somebody to pick me up. A guy my age. The son of one of the men he works with. A guy named Sam.

"Forget it, Dad."

2

"Try to be nice to the guy, okay? Got to go. Bye."

When I called back, he didn't pick up. I left a message, telling him there was no way I was going to let this guy give me a ride home. I'd take a taxi instead.

When I finally boarded my flight, I was assigned an aisle seat in the same row with a mom and her two kids, one a baby and the other a girl maybe eight years old. Across the aisle were the dad and two more kids, a boy maybe ten and a girl about three.

"What's your name?" the girl asked when I sat down.

"Charlene but people call me Charly," I said.

"My name is Kathleen but people call me Katie."

I smiled. "Good. So we got a lot in common. Where are you going today?"

"We're going to see our grandparents!" she said.

"Great! I bet they'll be happy to see you!"

"They will. We are their pride and joy. They tell us that all the time."

"I can see why, Katie. You'd be anybody's pride and joy."

She smiled. "Do you have any kids?"

"No, not yet."

"You should have some."

"You've been talking to my mom, right?" I said, glancing over at Katie's mom. She smiled. She knew what I was talking about. (Brown hair, blue eyes, great smile, not much makeup).

"Katie, let's color in your book," the mom said.

I opened my book and started to read.

Things went well for about an hour. But by that time Katie and her mom had gone through her books and puzzles. Also, the mom had to nurse her baby.

Katie wasn't happy. "I don't have anything to do," she said.

"Do another puzzle."

"I'm tired of doing puzzles."

"There's word games too in the book."

"I hate word games. When are we going to be there?"

I decided to see if I could help out. I grabbed my sketch pad from my back pack. "Katie, what would you like me to draw for you?"

She looked at me skeptically the way my art teachers often do.

"C'mon, give me a chance. I can draw anything."

"Can you draw an elephant?" she asked.

"Of course Elephants are. easy!"

I drew an elephant except I put him on a kid's bike.

She laughed. "Elephants can't ride bicycles!"

"Are you sure? Okay, if you say so. Let me try it again. I sure hope I get this one right."

That really made Katie laugh.

Her older brother Adam asked his mom if he
could switch seats. with her.

"Is that all right?" their mom asked me.

"Yeah, sure, no problem."

When we switched seats, the kids insisted I
be in the middle seat with Katie on my right and
Adam on my left.

We had a great time! I loved to make them laugh. This continued until we made our final approach to SLC. I gave them some of the sketches I'd done. They were so excited to have them. It made me realize I was spending way too much time around grumpy people.

After we landed, just before Katie and Adam and their family left, Katie threw her arms around me and told me she loved me.

"I love you too, Katie."

Adam gave me a hug too. Their mom, in the aisle, touched my shoulder and told me I was an answer to prayer. The dad nodded and said he was grateful for my being there. He seemed like a nice enough guy but, c'mon, who says grateful these days?

They left. On their way out Katie turned one more time and called out again that she'd never forget me.

I was having some rare stupid emotional moment so I let everyone else leave before me.

Why this reaction to being with two kids? For a short time there I'd felt, well, that kids are important, and that anyone who works with them, like their teachers, or their aunts, or, yes, their moms and dads are doing a great service. I know everyone in the world knows that but it wasn't something I'd ever thought about before.

In those few hours, I was important to Katie and Adam. And, yes, even needed. Usually nobody needs me. Not that I want that of course. All I want these days is to be thought of as competent, which at the New York School of the Arts is impossible.

I was one of the last passengers to leave the plane. I was happy until I remembered my dad's call about having someone else pick me up. When I finally reached the baggage area I saw a guy about my age holding a sign with my name on it. When I was still quite a ways from him, I stopped to look him over.

My first reaction? Amusement mixed with pity. His long sleeved button-down gray shirt which, with the outside temp being 100 degrees, made him look, well, socially awkward. Also, this guy was probably a Mormon. My dad had a running list of things that irritated him living in a town with so many Mormons. The list started with politics and ended with the annoying cheerfulness of the people he worked with.

The guy looked harmless enough. I approached him. "Are you my ride?" I asked.

"I'm Utah. Welcome to Sam!" he blurted out.

"Hello, Utah."

"Sorry. Actually, you know what? My name isn't Utah. It's Sam."

"To me you'll always be Utah."

At this point I had only two goals, to get home to my folks' place, and to give Sam such a bad time that Dad would never again think about setting me up with a guy just because he hated Mark.

A few minutes later as Sam was trying to stuff my luggage into the trunk of his dad's sports car, I grabbed the keys in the lock of the trunk, got in on the driver's side, started the car and revved the engine. "C'mon, Utah, let's go!"

"What are you doing?" Sam asked.

"Get in!"

He slammed the trunk and ran over to the passenger side and got in.

I drove like a New Yorker which terrified poor Sam.

"Slow down! This is my dad's car and I'd like to borrow it again someday."

"Relax, okay? This is the way people drive in the City. Fun, huh?"

After twenty minutes of this, I was bored. Sam wasn't complaining anymore. He kept his head down so he couldn't see the way I was driving.

I saw a Ferris wheel at a park. I drove as close as I could get to it, parked, then jumped out and started running toward it.

Sam ran after me. "What are you doing?"

"Isn't this great?"

I slowed down so he could keep up with me. On our way to the ticket booth, I asked, "Did your dad give you any money to get you to pick me up at the airport?"

"Yes. Forty dollars."

"Give it to me please."

"Why?"

He gave me two twenties.

"We need to get tickets." I gave it all to the man. "Forty dollars worth of tickets."

"Why that much?" Sam asked.

"Because it's what I want to do."

Okay, I did feel a little sorry for him. Don't they teach guys in Utah to stand up for themselves?

I asked the old guy running the Ferris wheel what his name was.

"Raferty," he said.

"Mr. Raferty, I'd like you to meet my fiancé. He just proposed, and you're the first one we've told!"

Sam shook his head. "That's not true. Actually we just met."

"Congratulations, Kids."

"Why, thank you! Sam and I want to ride your Ferris wheel for a long, long time. You understand, don't you?"

He winked at me. "I sure do. I'm not that old."

We got in and our ride started. "So we're just going to sit here for...what...until it closes down?" Sam asked.

"That's right."

"What's going to happen when one of us has to go to the restroom, or have you even thought of that?"

"I haven't but I'm sure you have."

"Why do you say that?"

"Because that's what you do, right? Pop every balloon, dash every hope."

"You don't know anything about me," he said.

"Don't I? Why is your shirt buttoned all the way to the top? Why are you wearing a long-sleeve gray shirt in July? You don't think that tells people something about yourself?"

"Oh, yeah, well I got a question for you."

"Okay."

He blushed. "What you're wearing."

"That's not a question."

"If I wanted to, I could see your belly button."

"If you don't want to see my belly button, don't look."

"I don't want to see it and I'm not looking."

"You must have looked at least once to see that it wasn't covered."

"Well, yea, but just for a second."

"You should be ashamed of yourself!"

"Me? What about you?"

We'd both had it with each other. "Okay, I give up," I said. "Me getting so many tickets was a dumb idea, wasn't it?"

"That's one thing we can both agree on."

"Do you want to see if we can get our money back?" I asked.

"Since when did it become our money?"

"Okay, your dad's money. So, did he pay you to pick me up?"

"Yeah, basically."

"I'm not taking that personally. He doesn't even know me."

"If he did, he'd have given me a lot more."

I started laughing. I'm sure he didn't know what to make of that. Sarcasm is something I can deal with. It's sincerity that kills me.

He shook his head. "I don't know how to take you."

I leaned into him. "Take me where?" I whispered in my sexiest voice, which only makes me sound like I have a bad cold.

He backed away. "What's that about?"

"You want to be a father, Utah?" I whispered in his ear.

He started to blush. "What?"

"A dad. A father of children. You want to propagate your species?"

He moved away. "Not today, thank you very much! And not with you."

" C'mon, work with me here. This is me being curious. After you get married, are you going to want to have kids?"

"Yes, of course."

"How many?"

"I don't know. Four or five maybe. It depends on my wife."

"Let me give you some advice. Call your first girl Katie, and your first son Adam. Okay?"

"Why?"

"Katie is a girl I met on the plane, along with her mom and her dad and her brother Adam and a baby girl. I made Katie and Adam laugh. It was so much fun. Best flight I've ever had."

Yes, Adam, now you know why we decided to name you Adam. I love the name, and I love you!   Mom

"So what?"

"Nothing ."

He shrugged his shoulders and with a slight smile said, "Good, I'm glad we could talk about this. I'm sure I was a big help to you."

"Okay, here's the deal. I'm practically engaged to this guy but, the thing is, he doesn't want to have kids. I mean ever. He's okay with a cat though."

"You two are almost engaged and you've never talked about this before?"

"No, not really, because there's a lot of things I want to get done in the next few years...graduate study...developing a portfolio...selling my work. All that takes time. Time I wouldn't have if I were a mom."

"So you and this guy are both in agreement about not having kids?"

"We were, I guess, until today, I was. Until Katie and her brother Adam came into my life, with their mom and dad looking mostly happy with their kids. They were coming to Utah so the kids could visit their grandparents. So I guess they're Mormons like you, right?"

"Probably so."

"Are you planning to go that route? Marriage? Family? Kids?"

"Yeah, I am."

"Got anyone in mind to marry?"

"No, not yet."

"Let me guess. A domestic type, right? Always willing to cook for you, clean for you, have your babies, and never complain. Am I right so far?"

"I don't know what I want but believe me she won't tell lies to complete strangers that we're engaged when we've just met each other."

"I don't just lie to complete strangers. I lie to my friends too."

"And she won't be parading around showing off her belly button either."

"What is it with you and belly buttons anyway?"

"Nothing. Which reminds me. I need to take a restroom break."

I leaned over. "Mr. Raferty, can you stop this thing? Sam here needs to go potty. I told him to go before we left, but you know how kids are, right?"

Mr. Raferty stopped and let us out. "You two coming back?" he asked.

I looked at Sam for the answer.

"We'll be back," he said, which surprised me.

As we walked off together, I asked Sam, "You could have ended this now, so why didn't you?"

He smiled. "I want my dad's money's worth."

"You interest me too."

He looked threatened. "I do?"

"Relax. It's nothing personal. In third grade I talked my dad into letting me go with a beekeeper when he was harvesting honey. So far you're coming in second to that. And with the bees I got stung twice, so don't get your hopes up too high."

We found and used the respective facilities and then joined up again.

"You want something to eat?" he asked.

"Yeah, I do."

"What?"

"A couple of hot dogs, an order of sweet potato fries, a large Cobb salad, and some iced tea."

He looked confused. "That much, huh?"

"It's two hours later for me. I got up in Eastern time."

He nodded. "Oh, sure. I'm not actually sure where we could get sweet potato fries here."

"What were you thinking of having?" I asked him.

"Hamburger, regular fries, and a drink."

"That'll work for me."

He drove me to a mom and pop café. They seemed to like him and they made a big fuss over me. I liked being there.

And then we went back to the park, took a long walk then returned to Mr. Raferty.

"You two love birds back for more?" he asked.

I thought Sam would set him straight but he didn't. "We are. We can't get enough of each other."

"I can see that."

Once we were moving again, I said, "What you said to Mr. Raferty surprised me."

"I was just kidding."

"I know. But, seriously, what would be your number one reason for not wanting to marry me? The fact that I hi-jacked your dad's car? My reckless driving? Exposing my belly button to the entire world? Stealing the tomato on your hamburger when you weren't looking? Which one?"

"You stole my tomato?" he asked with a faked sad look.

"Word to the wise, my friend. Never turn your back on a tomato in my presence."

"You want the number one reason why I'd never marry you?" He smiled. "Gosh, there's so many but the first one is that I will never marry someone who isn't a member of my church."

"I've got standards too, Utah. For example, I'd never marry someone who..." I stopped.

"Yes?" he asked.

"Who has no appreciation for art."

He faked being insulted. "And you think I don't?"

"Name a famous painting by Picasso."

He flashed me a stupid grin. "That's easy. The Moaning Lisa."

"And could you tell me more about that painting, Professor?" I asked.

"Yes, but take notes. The Moaning Lisa is about a woman named Lisa who is very sad because she lost her poodle Pixie Dust, or as we say in French, Peek-say Dooost."

It was totally lame but I laughed anyway.

"Tell me about your wedding day," I said.

"My bride and I will get married in one of our temples."

"I've heard they're beautiful buildings."

"That's not the reason. If you get married in a temple, it will last forever."

"What do you mean forever?"

"I mean even after you and your husband die, you'll still be married."

"You mean dead and married?"

"Yes."

"And having relations?"

"Yeah, sure, why not?"

"Just one problem. No body."

"We'll get new ones when we're resurrected."

"So basically you're hoping for a marriage that never dies."

"Right."

"I like the concept. Don't believe it but I like it."

After we'd finished eating we rode the Ferris wheel. When it was the end of Mister Raferty's shift, we gave it up.

Sam took me home. I didn't want him to meet my folks because I didn't want them to know I'd had a good time. I wanted to punish them. So I had him drop me off. He carried my bags to the porch though.

"Thanks. I had a great day. Can I take you to dinner sometime?" I asked.

"I guess so."

"Tomorrow at seven?" I asked.

"Okay."

"You'll pick me up?"

"I will. Not in my dad's car though."

"I agree. We need to get our dads totally out of this," I said.

"By the way, why are we doing this?" he asked. "In case my folks ask."

"Why would they care?"

"Well, they might worry about me spending time with a non-Mormon because if we got serious, we couldn't get married in the temple."

"Got it," I said. "So what could we do that would drive my folks crazy but make your mom and dad totally okay with it?"

"We could tell them that you want to know more about the Church and that I'm taking you to Temple Square for a tour of the Visitor's Center."

"Perfect! That will definitely set my folks off! Good job, Utah!"

"Okay then, we're set."

As he left, I called out to him. "I actually do respect you."

"Thanks," he said, and then drove off.

The polite thing of course would have been for him to say he respected me too. But he didn't. I know why too. It was because of my belly button.

That night after complaining to my mom and dad about them interfering with my life by having Sam pick me up, as I was getting ready for bed, I started to feel that in some small way I'd cheated on Mark. Not because I had any interest in Sam. He is way too non-cosmopolitan for me. But, even so, I am beginning to have some small amount of respect for him.

TUESDAY

Mark called. It was good to hear about his day. He did his usual thing of mocking his co-workers. That had always been hilarious to me before but this time it occurred to me that Sam wouldn't do that.

I told him about the Mormon guy who picked me up at the airport.

"You're not going to see him again?"

"What do you think?"

"Good. Oh, by the way, going to bed isn't half as much fun as when you're here."

"It better not be."

After our call I felt guilty I hadn't told Mark that Sam and I were going out to dinner today. But I decided I didn't owe anybody an explanation. Not my mom and dad, not Mark, not Sam, and not Granny.

Also, I feel a little guilty for not having told Sam that Mark and I are living together. It's not that I'm ashamed, and for sure I'll tell Sam if it ever comes up. It's just that when you first meet someone, it's not something you bring up. Besides, I did tell Sam that I was practically engaged so he ought to know what that means. In NYC he'd know, but maybe not here.

In the afternoon I helped Granny get ready for her art exhibit which is scheduled in August. There are a thousand details that still need to be worked out: catering, invitations, publicity. Things I 'm good at.

When I was growing up, I took Granny for granted. But not anymore. She's always been on my side. And, of course, it was from her I developed my love for art.

I asked Granny if maybe one or two of my paintings could be included in her show. She smiled. "Well, of course. I just hope people will pay some attention to my work once they see yours."

Neither of us believed that of course.

"I didn't bring any of my latest ones with me but I'll start on some new ones and you can tell me if there's any you like."

"Very good."

Mom and Dad had recently put a couple of my paintings in the living room so I was a little bummed out she didn't offer to show those. I mean I am her grand-daughter. But I knew she had to be careful because it was her show.

After we were done for the day I jogged around the neighborhood then took a shower and got ready to be with Sam. Picking out what I was going to wear wasn't easy. At one point I had five different outfits on the bed, trying to decide which one wouldn't set off alarm bells with Sam.

This is ridiculous, I thought. What do I care what he thinks? After tonight I'll never see him again.

I decided to stay in my room until he came. I wanted to cut the explaining to a minimum.

Finally I heard the doorbell ring. "I'll get it," I said as I hurried to our front door.

"Who's at the door?" my mom asked.

"Sam, the guy who picked me up at the airport, the one Dad set me up with. He's taking me to the Temple Square Visitor's Center. I told him I wanted to know what Mormons believe."

"Why do you want to know what Mormons believe?" Dad asked with that edge in his voice he gets when he's mad.

"It's what tourists here do, Dad."

Dad frowned. "Mormons don't drink coffee."

You got to be kidding, I thought. But for the purposes of rattling my parents' cage, I said, "How interesting! I'm sure I'll learn this and many other fascinating things in the religious indoctrination I receive today."

That got to Dad big time! Good.

Sam rang the bell again.

"Let me get this, okay?" I opened the door. "Sam, come in and meet my family."

He looked intimidated as he stepped inside.

"This is my mom and my dad and my grandmother. "Just call 'em Eddy and Clair. They like that." They grimaced.

Granny got a silly smile on her face and placed her hand on his chest. "You can call me anything you want."

Sam started to blush at the inappropriate attention he was getting from Granny.

"Sam, why don't you tell me that fascinating thing about humidity you told me yesterday?" I asked.

"There's a difference in humidity between Utah and New York."

My folks stared at him.

"We have less humidity here...and they have more humidity in New York," he continued.

Absolute silence.

"So that's why you say there's a difference in humidity," I said, trying not to laugh.

He nodded. "That's why you feel so uncomfortable now," he said.

"I don't feel uncomfortable," I said.

"Wait until we get outside."

I moved closer and spoke seductively in his ear, "You mean when I'm all alone with you in your car late at night?"

He blushed. "That's not what I meant."

That set Dad off. "What did you mean?"

I turned and smiled. "Don't wait up for us. Who knows how long we'll be?"

After we'd driven a few blocks, he goes, "What was that all about?"

"You mean me saying what was going to happen when I was alone with you? That's pay-back to my dad."

"Oh. Do you always do pay back?"

"Yes, I always do pay back. I'm from New York, okay? That's what we do there."

"I see," he said softly. I knew I'd blown it again.

He took me to the Visitor's Center at Temple Square and we walked around. I tried to zone out on the doctrine and just appreciate the art work. My goal was look mildly interested, and I think I carried that off quite well.

Only once did the place get to me and that was when we were coming downstairs to the first floor. I stopped on the stairs and looked out and saw entire families-- moms, dads, and their kids. For a second I thought I saw Katie and Adam and their mom and dad. I wanted to run down and say hello to them but then I realized it wasn't them.

Families, I thought. Whole families. What a great idea.

Sam noticed. "You okay?"

I nodded. "Yeah. I'm good. Oh, not good like you, of course, but you get the idea."

We ended up at the reflection pool just outside Temple Square. A little kid had a sail boat and by mistake he pushed it too hard and it started going out toward the middle. He started crying.

His dad had no sympathy for the poor kid. . "We told you to be careful! Well, we can't get it now. Maybe some other boy will get it later today. I just hope he takes better care of it than you did."

The poor kid cried even more. I felt sorry for him.

"Hey, Kid, don't worry, okay?" I said. I took off my shoes, hiked up my dress, and walked into the water toward the boat. I heard a small splash of water and turned to see that Sam was right behind me. That impressed me because I'd never seen Mark go out of his way to help a stranger. We retrieved the boat then returned. "Here you go," I said, giving the kid his boat.

"What do you say?" his mom asked.

"Thank you!" He gave both Sam and me a big hug.

"No problem. We were glad to help out," I said.

Adam, your dad helped me get that kid's toy boat. I'd never before known a guy like that before. I hope you will always look for opportunities to help others. Also I want you to know what a great dad you've got. Love, Mom

Just then a security cop shows up, telling us that wading in the pool is not allowed.

The kid's mom came to the rescue. "My son let his boat get away from him. These two went in and got it for us."

The cop smiled. "Oh, well, that's different! Good job!" He patted Sam on the shoulder and then moved on.

"We need to find restrooms so we can blow-dry our clothes," I said to Sam. "Let's go back to the Visitor's Center."

It took me ten minutes and a few weird stares as I used the hand dryer on my dress. And then I joined Sam and he took me to a restaurant across from the temple. He got us a table where we had a good view of the temple.

I made the mistake of calling Temple Square the Mormon Vatican. Sam didn't appreciate that. He also didn't appreciate me sampling a few things off his plate. And when I asked the waitress for a glass of wine, he didn't appreciate that either. She told me they don't serve alcoholic beverages. How would I know that?

I desperately needed some kind of approval from the guy so I asked if he was pleased he couldn't see my belly button. "Better than yesterday, right?" I said with a big hearty chuckle.

He blushed and looked around to see if anyone was listening in.

I realized with some relief that this was all about to end. He'd picked me up at the airport like his dad had asked. And now I was taking him to dinner to thank him for that. So that's it. We're done. There's no reason for us to see each other again.

I'm not sure why that was a little disappointing. Maybe it was dreading spending every evening for the next month at home with my mom and dad listening to them argue. While in Utah I could use a guy to hang out with but not feel guilty (because of Mark) for seeing him. He'd be like a life preserver in a storm.

It's not like I'm hiding anything from Sam. I already told him that Mark and I are practically engaged. He probably thinks that means we're about to get married. But of course that's not what it means.

I asked Mark once about us getting married. He said he wasn't ready for that yet. Actually, when I thought about it, I decided I wasn't either.

But still it makes me wonder how committed he is to me. I could see him getting tired of me sometime in the future. Or me getting tired of him. And then what? I find someone else for a while? And where does it end? One doomed relationship after another?

With Katie and Adam, their mom and dad are married. And they'll stay that way because they love their kids. If they have problems, they'll try to work them out.

I have no interest in hooking up with Sam. The last thing either of us would want would be to get romantically involved. But even so, maybe we could be friends for a while.

"While I'm here, I'd like to learn more about..."

Awkward alert. *Don't say you,* I thought.

"More about your church."

He got a big smile on his face. "I think I can make that happen."

Saved by religion. That's a first for me.

WEDNESDAY

I have never been more uncomfortable in my life than being taught by two Mormon missionaries, Sister Smith and Sister Weston, with Sam sitting next to me on their living room couch, his Mormon scriptures in hand.

How it worked was they had me read something from their Bible-like books and then they'd ask me a question for which there was only one answer, the answer they wanted me to give.

I'm not someone who can play that game. But instead of saying something hilariously funny that would later make me feel bad for trashing these two...uh, sisters, I pretended not to know the answer. When I did that, they'd say that's okay and then have Sam answer the question. Everyone felt good about themselves so it worked fairly well.

So finally, mercifully, it was over. They asked me to pray. I said I'd rather not. So they asked who I'd like to pray. I went with Sister

Weston. We knelt down. She prayed that I'd come to "know the truth of the things we'd discussed today."

I thought that was putting a big burden on God because I didn't even want to know if it was true.

After the prayer, I stood up and with a big smile said, "So, basically, all churches are good, right?"

Sam frowned and the sisters looked discouraged.

And then we had what Mormons call refreshments. Strawberry shortcake! Sam's mom had made. It tasted great!

Eating shortcake gave me a chance to get to know Smith and Weston. For one thing Smith called her Wesson, but when she introduced herself she said her name was Weston. So I asked about that.

"Have you ever heard of Smith and Wesson?" Sister Smith asked me.

"No."

"They manufacture guns. So that's what the elders started calling us."

"Elders?"

"Guy missionaries," Sister Weston said. "The elders started calling us Smith and Wesson."

"I'll always call you by your real name," I said.

Smith and Weston asked if they could schedule a time for them to teach me again. I told them I was going to be busy helping my grandmother set up an art exhibit but if they'd give me their number, I'd call them when I had some free time.

They wanted to know about the art exhibit so I told them, adding I would also probably be showing some of my work.

They invited me to church. I backed out of that as well.

Smith and Weston gave me a copy of the Book of Mormon and their phone number and then left. Sam offered to show me their backyard, which is like a small farm.

So he's showing me around and I'm asking what they do with all this stuff, and he says we can it, which makes no sense to me. So he has to explain that to me too.

But then I discover the raspberries. So I'm munching through their crop when he asks me what I thought about the discussion and I tell him I didn't believe a word of it.

We talk for a while and then he asks if I'd like to pray with him about it.

"Where? Here?" And then I do my version of prayer. "Hey, God, you up there?"

He says "Something like that."

He kneels down and asks me to kneel down with him, which I do.

So there he is on his knees, his eyes closed, his arms folded.

He opens his eyes and sees me staring at him.

"Sam, you're definitely crazy."

I stand up. "Thank your mom for the dessert. I loved it." I grab a small handful of raspberries for the trip home. I decide to not go through the house to get to my car.

He calls out after me. "By their fruits ye shall know them!"

Okay, that was actually a clever thing to say.

I was almost to my car when he caught up with me. "Sorry," he said. "I shouldn't have tried to get you to pray with me."

"You think? Look, I happen to know all the ways to lead a guy along, and me making you think I'm interested in your church when I'm definitely not is one of those ways. I can't do that. I respect you and your mom and dad and Smith and Weston too much for that."

He nodded.

"So I guess this is the end of the trail for us, Pardner," I said.

"I guess so."

As I was getting into my car, he came over, "Wait. There's one more thing we could do to spend time together that my mom and dad would be okay with."

"What's that?"

"I could take you fishing."

"Good idea, Utah, because I have absolutely no interest in fishing."

He nodded proudly. "Exactly."

"I'll tell you what. I'll go fishing with you one time. .That means our ill-fated friendship isn't over yet."

"Looks that way."

We were staring at each other and then for no reason, we both broke into big cheesy grins.

I have no idea what that was about.

THURSDAY

This morning I had Granny look at a painting I'd just finished. It was of some fruit I found in our kitchen.

For a long time she didn't say anything.

"So, what do you think?" I asked.

"Technically, it's fine. But why the fruit salad? What's so compelling about a bunch of fruit?"

"My style is different than yours."

"It's not about style. This is an exercise. Until you feel something here, (she put her hand about where my heart is), you can't reveal it here." (She touched the canvas).

"You're right. It's your show. I'm just not ready yet."

"Find something you feel so deeply about that you're not sure you can paint it. Then go ahead and do it."

I felt devastated.

A few minutes later I packed up all the paintings I'd ever done, including two from the kitchen. I drove to the city dump. I pulled up to the edge where people dump their junk. There was a beat-up old pickup not far from where I was with an old man shoveling stuff out the back.

I opened the trunk of my mom's car and pulled out my most recent painting of fruit and vegetables and two more I'd done a few years earlier that I'd taken from the kitchen. And then I flung it into the garbage pit like it was a Frisbee.

"What are you doing?" the man asked me.

"I'm starting over!"

I picked up another painting.

He came over to look at it. "It's a shame to waste a nice painting like that."

"It's just fruit."

"It's very realistic though! That looks just like the banana I had for breakfast this morning!"

He couldn't have said anything worse. With a karate shout, I flung it into the garbage pit and then reached for my last painting.

"Can I have that one?" he asked.

"No. I've got to get rid of everything in my life that isn't working. Like this!" I launched it and got back in my car and drove away.

I wasn't much good to Granny in the afternoon. I went back to my room and sulked. Right now I'm thinking the worst thing that can happen is to have a grandmother tell you when you're growing up how talented you are. After a while you start to believe it.

And why wouldn't I believe her? She's a world-class artist. So I believed her and I went to college and I worked as hard as I could and I'm just about to graduate and then today I find out I don't have what it takes, so now what do I do?

All I wanted was to have one stupid painting of mine in her show.

She says I need to feel so deeply about something that I'm not sure I can paint it. Then do it.

So that brings up a question I've never asked myself before. What do I feel deeply about?

I got nothing. Zip. Nada.

What about Mark? Do I feel strongly about him? Well, in the first place, he's a person not an idea. Do I feel strongly about an idea, a concept, a principle?

I try to come up with something but in the end I still got nothing.

But, you know what? While we're on the topic, what are the good things about Mark? He makes me laugh. We get along. We have similar lifestyles. We're both living in NYC.

He says I'm good for him, but why is that? Is it because I make no demands on him? Or is it because I'm always available for him?

What am I doing with my life? Where am I going? In many ways I'm just like a piece of fruit in a stupid fruit bowl. I make no demands of the bowl, and the bowl makes no demands of me.

Feel something deeply about? What is that about? Some people are just shallow. Maybe I'm one of them. What am I going to do? Quit? Start over?

I don't know. I've hit bottom.

Adam, I hope this never happens to you but sometime in your life you may hit bottom and realize you need to start over. As you can see, this happened to me. So do what I did and don't give up.! Just start over! You can do it!

I love you!

Mom

LATER, SAME DAY

Okay, I'm done feeling sorry for myself. I just need to start over and reinvent myself. I hate it that I have to do that though. I liked being shallow and two-dimensional with no depth. Like my stupid fruit-bowl art.

SATURDAY

I can see why Sam likes fishing. It's because it's almost as boring as he is.

We were just sitting there each watching our fishing line. And about a hundred feet away were two other boats with the people in them doing the same.

Since Sam wasn't talking to me, I stood up and tried to start a conversation with the people in one of the other boats.

They wouldn't talk to me. Sam told me that normally people don't talk between boats.

I couldn't take it anymore. So that meant it was time to yank Sam's chain.

"So why don't people talk between boats?"

"It scares the fish."

"Give me a spear gun and a mask. I'll show you 'scare the fish.'"

He smiled politely.

I stood up and did a bit for the other fisher people around me. It was about me being with the Utah Fish and Game Department (UFGD) and saying that some fishermen have been using marshmallows to attract the fish and that a recent study showed that the fish in this lake have fifty-three percent more cavities. I asked if they knew what this meant.

They of course didn't respond.

I told them that now the UFGD must stand the expense of sending a trout through dental school.

Silence. Absolute silence.

I started laughing. "A trout through dental school! That is good! In fact it's hilarious! What is wrong with you people?"

"Charly?"

"Yes."

"Please sit down and be quiet."

I sat down and cast my line as far as I could. And snagged a fish!

After we got it in, I stood up and tried to continue my comedy bit but Sam started rowing us away as fast as he could.

He admitted I'd embarrassed him.

I accused him of having no sense of fun. He claimed that he laughed. I told him what he did was smile faintly. He goes I laugh responsibly.

I took my water bottle and threw some water on his face. He kept rowing.

I go, "No, Sam, you're supposed to throw water on me now. It's what we call a water fight. Can you say that for me, Sweetheart? Wa...ter...fight."

I was so mad at him I wanted to throw him into the lake.

Which, actually, did happen. But it wasn't my fault.

I grabbed his cell phone and threatened to throw it in the water. I dropped it thinking I'd grab it just before it hit the water but he lunged for it, lost his balance and fell into the water. But much to his credit he did catch his cell phone before he went into the water with it.

I was laughing so hard! Him not so much.

I was afraid he'd push me in after he got back in the boat. So I rowed back to shore before I let him back in the boat. It wasn't that far for him to swim. So I acted as his swimming coach. "Come on, Sam, you can do it! Don't give up now! We're almost there."

When we turned in our rental boat and even on our way back to SLC, he did not speak to me. When I told him it wasn't my fault, he just glared at me.

Once in SLC, he drove to where he bought the phone to see if his warranty would cover what had happened.

He was still wet when we entered the big-box store. He was mad at me even though I insisted it wasn't my fault.

I figured he'd probably never want to do anything with me again. So, really, I had nothing to lose. I went to the manager and told him I'd lost my little boy in the store and asked if I could use the store intercom.

49

"Sam, Sammy, this is Mommy. Remember when we came last week and I bought you popcorn. Come to the popcorn machine and Mommy has a big bag of popcorn for you. Please, Sammy, go to the popcorn machine. If you can't remember where it is, ask one of the nice people who work here. Mommy loves you!"

I went and bought some popcorn and waited for him.

He had a strange expression on his face.

"Sam, I said I was sorry, didn't I? So we're good, right?"

He picked me up and carried me out of the store.

And he laughed on our way to his car. I mean a real gut laugh.

You know what? I couldn't have been happier.

SUNDAY, JUNE 15

I thought about going to some random church this morning but not where Sam goes. I didn't want him to be hopeful.

Actually any denomination would do. I asked Granny if she wanted to go with me but she said no. So I went to my room and opened the Book of Mormon the sisters had given me and started reading.

I read for a couple of hours.

I actually like it that Nephi whacked Laban and then stole his brass Bible. When the most righteous guy you know has whacked a guy and stolen his expensive Bible, it sort of makes your sins seem hardly worth mentioning. It's like, "Dear God, okay I told a lot of lies today to make myself look good but, c'mon, cut me some slack here. At least I didn't whack anyone and steal his Bible, if you catch my drift. Amen."

I thought about telling Sam that I'm reading the Book of Mormon. But I won't because I'm afraid he'll get crazy on me again like when he tried to get me to pray with him in the backyard.

After lunch I called Smith and Weston and asked if they could teach me again, and if we could do it without Sam. It's none of his business what I do.

So about seven that night I drove to the Mormon Church near where they lived. I parked in the back. The sisters were in their car waiting for me. They had keys that got us in. We went to a classroom and they taught me.

It was okay I guess. But actually it's almost too much to take in. A prophet in New York State in the eighteen hundreds? How could this have happened and so few know about it? I don't get it. I took New York State history in school. Why is this the first time I'm hearing all this?

One thing I liked about this experience was it gave me a chance to learn more about the sisters.

Smith is from Montana. She was born and raised on a ranch. She can actually rope cows, at least that's what she said. She doesn't use much makeup but truth is she doesn't need to. She's a natural beauty.

Weston is from South Philly. She's a convert. She was baptized two years ago. She's always saying things that only an Easterner would get. That makes her easy for me to like.

I told them that I'd started reading the Book of Mormon.

That made them happy. They asked if I had any questions. I said I'd like to know how to pronounce all the names. They showed me a pronouncing guide and we went through all the major names I'm going to come across in my reading.

At the end they asked me to pray. I told them I couldn't do that. I didn't know how. They said they'd teach me.

Smith taught me their basic format. It started with Father in Heaven.

I go, "Why is God my father?"

Weston goes that it's because before you were born you existed and knew God as your Father...not just you...but everyone who's ever lived or who will ever live.

"You're talking spiritual essence like a vapor, right?" I asked.

"No, a father you could go to. That's how we knew him before we were born."

"And sit on his lap?"

"We don't have any details about that but Father in Heaven is the kind of father you'd want to sit on his lap."

"So how can he be my father? Was I born before I came to earth?"

"We suppose so."

"So is there a mom too up there?"

"Yes."

"How do you people know all this and nobody else does?"

"I think you know the answer to that question."

"Prophets, right?"

"Good job."

Weston left and came back with one of their hymnals and turned to a song called "Oh My Father." She read the verses and then went to the piano and we sang the whole thing a couple of times.

This was getting to me so I told them I had to go home.

They asked me again to pray and I said I would if they'd give me some help.

So I did it. And I think I did a good job, it being my first time.

They asked me to pray each time I sat down to read the Book of Mormon.

I asked why.

They said so Father in Heaven can give you an answer.

"What makes you think He'll do that?"

They had me read a promise near the back of the book. It could be interpreted I guess as saying that if you ask God with real intent about the Book of Mormon, he'll give you an answer.

My first thought was, Does God know these two chicks are going around town promising people what God is going to do for them? And, more important, will God come through for them?

You know what? If I were God, I totally would.

But it hasn't happened yet.

MONDAY, JUNE 16

Mark called today. He says he's got to fly to L.A. for business in a few days. He wants to arrange his schedule so he'll have a stay-over in SLC. He'll book a room for us so we can have some alone time together. He says that will get him over the drought he's experiencing with me gone.

That should have made me happy but it didn't. Not because I've adopted the Mormon concept of chastity either. It's something else. I started thinking, Is this the only thing we've got going for us? In the six months we've been living together has he ever said he loves me? No, not once. He says we have a good thing going though. But he could say that to his barber, right?

If what we've got together isn't love, what is it? Convenience?

And another thing. If what we have is, for him, only about making love then when we break up, will I feel depressed and perhaps even cheated out of something that should have had more meaning?

I told Mark that I'm too busy now helping Granny get ready for her exhibit.

That made him so mad he hung up on me. No surprise there. He's got a bit of a temper when he doesn't get his way.

Poor baby.

TUESDAY

This started out as just another sketch pad for things I see each day. But now it's become a diary of sorts. And things are happening to me that are important to record, like being taught by the Sisters and becoming friends with Sam, and trying to change what I choose to paint.

So I've torn out the pages up to the day I met Sam. So now this is my official diary.

Why do this? I seem to be changing and I need to keep a record of that.

So, bottom line, from now on I'm going to use this as a kind if diary.

The sisters taught me again. I told them about Mark and me, that we had lived together until I came out here to live. They had me read some passages in their scriptures that basically says that sex is reserved for marriage. I guess I'd sort of come to that conclusion from my last phone conversation with Mark.

I asked them to tell me everything else Mormons are supposed to avoid so they gave me the whole list. Not only what they stay away from but also the positive things they're supposed to do.

No coffee, no wine, no tea, no drugs, no sex outside marriage, no swearing. Go to church for three hours every Sunday. Three hours? And fast once a month for 24 hours and donate the money you saved to the Church to help those who are needy. Give ten percent of your income to the church.

What is happening to me? It's like my whole life is crumbling away. Sometimes I just want to go back to the garbage dump, pick up my stupid fruit paintings and return to my old familiar lifestyle.

The good thing about being shallow is you know all the answers.

Maybe that's the problem.

I guess they could tell how I was feeling. They suggested we read out loud a few verses from the Book of Mormon, starting with Chapter Eleven of Third Nephi. We read through Chapter Eighteen.

By the time we'd finished reading, I'd lost it totally. It was the closest I'd ever felt to Jesus. Especially when he asked if they had any sick among them and then had them brought to him. And then he healed them one by one. People who were blind, deaf, crippled, maimed. It didn't matter. He healed them all. Every one of them.

I needed to get out of there. I asked one of them to pray for me.

Smith did. While she was praying for me, I started crying. But I didn't want them to know so I wiped away my tears like crazy.

After the prayer Weston asked if I was okay. I said, Yeah, sure, why wouldn't I be?

The rest of the week I was busy helping Granny. But I started thinking about a new painting.

SATURDAY

In the morning Sam and I climbed to the top of some mountain. Right before we reached the top, it got dangerously steep. Sam grabbed my hand and pulled me up with him. Once we reached the top, we stood there looking out at what we could see from there, but still holding hands, until he cleared his throat awkwardly (as is his custom) and let go of my hand.

So what's that all about? Was he holding my hand only because he's like CAPTAIN SAFETY ON THE TRAILS GUY? Or was it something else?

I'm sure I'll never know, and I'm certainly not going to ask.

That should have been enough for one day but on our way back, he asked if I'd like to go to a zoo. I said I would. And so that's what we did.

The place was packed. And all the time we were there, I couldn't help looking at the kids and their moms and dads. What is it with me these days? This has never happened to me before. Always before getting pregnant would be the worst possible thing that could happen to me. But now, if I were married, I can see that having a kid might be a good thing.

Married to a guy like Sam? I don't know. For sure he's a good enough guy, and there's so few of them out there these days.

SUNDAY, JUNE 22

Went to church with the sisters. The first thing I did when I met them in the parking lot was to ask them if what I was wearing was okay. After a slight pause, Weston sighed and said it was okay. Which gave me the answer to my question. It wasn't okay.

What do these people want from me anyway? At least my belly button wasn't showing.

After church they gave me another lesson.

MONDAY

My mom and dad and Granny were all out of the house in the afternoon. I asked the sisters to come over and help me go through my clothes to see which ones would be okay for church. Of course I hadn't brought all my clothes from my apartment in NYC but there were quite a few things that the movers had just packed up at our old house in NJ when my folks moved west--some of the clothes going back to when I was in high school.

By the time we'd finished, I had a big pile of clothes to give to charity. I kept back a few things though just in case I ever decide to revert back to my old self.

I've got an idea for a tourist promotion for the state of Utah: COME TO UTAH AND LOSE YOUR IDENTITY! That's what seems to be happening to me. My only question is will there be anything left of me when I'm done.
WEDNESDAY

The sisters taught me tonight in what they call the Relief Society room.

I'd asked a question. Smith was trying to answer it. First we look up a passage in the New Testament, and then we go to the Book of Mormon, and then to something else called the Doctrine and Covenants.

I'm not sure if I was following it all. Probably not. But while they were both doing this, I looked at them and the thought came to me that these two would never be part of something that wasn't true. They believe it. And I trust them, actually more than anyone I've ever known.

So then I start thinking, maybe this is true after all.

Once I thought that, an amazing calm peaceful feeling came over me.

Maybe that's it, I thought. What they've been telling me it would be like to feel the Spirit.

They paused. "Does that answer your question?"

"Read to me the promise, the one in the Book of Mormon."

She read it.

"Okay, let me ask you something else? Am I eligible for this promise to come true?"

Weston goes, "Have you asked Father in Heaven if it's true with real intent, having faith in Christ?"

"I have asked. And I am serious when I ask it, and I ask God every day."

"Then you're eligible."

"Okay, you two do know I was living with a guy before I came out here, right?"

"You told us that."

"And you do know what living together means, right?"

"We do,"

"So why doesn't that matter to God?"

"Because you're not doing that now. Besides, what will count for you from now on is what you do after you're baptized. Because when you're baptized, all your sins are washed away and forgiven."

"Wait! In grade school I used to steal candy bars from a store. I never got caught either. I was so good at it! I could show you both sometime how I did it."

I noticed their expressions. "Oh, sorry."

"Doesn't matter. Once you're baptized, all your sins are washed away."

"How about giving me a couple of weeks to go on a sinning holiday, and then I'll be baptized."

Their mouths dropped open. I had 'em on that one.

"Just kidding."

They seemed relieved.

"One more thing. In junior high I talked my dad into buying me a harp. It cost a fortune. Once I got it, I never practiced."

Weston threw her hands in the air. "Wats da matta witchew? You crossed the line with that one, Charly!"

I thought she was serious. "Really?" .

They both laughed. Weston goes, "No, of course not!" She says with a big grin on her face.

"Can we have like a group hug?" I asked

We did, and all three of us were crying but with big smiles on our faces.

"I love you both," I said.

"We love you too," Weston says.

"This has been the best experience of my mission," Smith says.

"I couldn't have had anyone better than you two to teach me. Way better than Sam."

"Are you going to ask him to baptize you?" Smith asks.

I shrugged my shoulders. "I don't know. I haven't thought about it. Neither one of you can baptize me, right?"

"No, we don't have the priesthood."

"To tell you the truth I don't know if I want Sam to baptize me."

"Why not?" Weston goes.

"If he baptizes me, he'll go around bragging to everyone about how I was his convert and how he made it happen. You know how guys are, right?"

They both started laughing.

"We know," Weston goes. "The missionary elders we work with, they always claim a little of the credit for every baptism we have."

I felt relieved they understood.

"One other thing. This is off the subject but I don't have anyone else to talk to. I've wanted Sam to kiss me for about a week, but he never has, maybe because he thinks he's better than me, like I'm not good enough for his precious lips to touch mine."

"Didn't you once tell him you were engaged?" Smith goes.

"I said practically engaged. That's not the same thing as engaged."

"If he thinks you're almost engaged, he's not going to kiss you."

"Yeah, I guess you're right. The guy has principles. Of all the rotten luck."

"When you told him you were practically engaged, did you say you were sleeping with the guy? " Weston asked

"No, I've never told him that."

"Are you going to?"

"I don't know. I guess I'm afraid if I do, he'll have nothing more to do with me."

"And you'd miss that?" Smith goes.

"Yes, I would. I'd miss that a lot."

"Why?"

"I know this is crazy. But I think I'm starting to fall for the guy. I know that doesn't make sense. But the thing is, he's a good guy. I've had guys before be considerate of me but that was only because they wanted to get me into bed. But that's not it with Sam. He's a one hundred percent nice guy. And now with a little coaching on my part, I can get him to actually laugh. So with a little help from me, there could be hope for him, you know what I mean?"

Smith smiled. "My mom once told me that for every bride it's like buying a new car that's only partially put together. You no sooner get one thing fixed when another flaw shows up."

We all laughed at that.

THURSDAY

I was on fire today! One great idea after another for my next project. I finally decided on one to work on. Everyone has seen Michelangelo's painting "The Creation of Adam", showing God's hand touching Adam. I'm thinking of using the same idea except it will be me and I'll be completely clothed.

Maybe it will be no good, but it's the way I feel now that I've been assured by the Spirit that the Book of Mormon is the word of God.

In some ways I'm surprised by the rush of ideas coming to me now. On first thought you'd think that a religion that imposes limits on what you can do would also put a limit on creativity. But exactly the opposite seems to be true, at least for me.

I told Granny this morning that I wanted to stay home today and work on my new project. She seemed excited for me.

I hope I can finish this in time for the opening of the exhibit which now is about two weeks away.

Sam invited me to have dinner with his family. They're having a mini family reunion so I'll get to meet his two older sisters and their kids. LATER

I don't know what it is about me and kids these days. They're so much fun to be with! At

Sam's house his nieces Emily, 11, and Becca, 9, and I got together and I did my bit about drawing anything in the world for them.

We had a great time. I love to hear kids laugh. At one point I looked over and noticed Sam taking this all in. He gave me a thumbs up and I smiled and nodded.

Yes, Sam, I would make a great wife and mom for your kids. Not that I'm applying for the job. Just wanted you to know.

Just before we left his house, I asked if we could go in the back yard.

"Why? You ate all our raspberries the first time you were here."

"I've got a big surprise for you!" I said with a big grin.

I guessed by his expression that he was worried I might show off my belly button to his entire family.

We went outside. Emily and Becca were still out there, on the swings.

I took him to the place where he had once tried to get me to pray with him.

70

"Let us pray," I said with great solemnity.

"What are you two doing?" Becca asked.

"We're going to pray," I said. "Want to join us?"

The two girls knelt down with us.

"I'll say the prayer," I said "Heavenly Father, it was here that Sam tried to help me start on a journey that would help me learn more about you...I mean thee. Well, now that journey is complete. I am so glad that I'm going to be baptized this Saturday. In the name of Jesus Christ. Amen."

Sam looked at me, not trusting he'd actually heard what I'd said.

"Come again?" he said.

"I'm going to be baptized Saturday. Will you baptize me?"

Sam jumped up, grabbed Emily's hand on one side, and my hand on the other side. I grabbed Becca's hand and we danced around in a circle laughing and crying together.

"Go get Grandaddy and Grandmother!" Sam said to the girls. "Tell them Charly is getting baptized! Bring them out here!"

It was so great to be hugged by everyone there, but especially to be hugged by Sam.

SATURDAY, JUNE 28, MY BAPTISM DAY

I can't even begin to describe the way it was for me to be baptized and confirmed. It was like a warm blanket on a cold night. It was like a cold glass of lemonade on a hot day. It was like the way you'd feel in the presence of God.

I had Sam baptize me and asked his dad to confirm me.

My mom and dad came. They were polite but I could tell they weren't happy with me becoming a Mormon. Granny came too. She seemed happy for me. She was friendly and gracious to everyone there. I was so grateful for her good attitude.

A few days before I decided to get baptized, I talked to Granny about it. She told me that if that's what I want then just go do it, but if I'm going to do it, be the best I can at it. Thanks, Granny, I love you!

Sam's mom brought strawberry shortcake for everyone to have after it was over. My mom and dad had some and then quickly left. I know they're not happy with me. I'll just have to give them some time, that's all.

Adam, as I write these notes to you, I picture you being in your early twenties and perhaps even being married. I want you to know that your birth mom died with a testimony that Jesus Christ is the Savior of the world, and that Joseph Smith was a prophet of God, and that the Book of Mormon is the word of God as much as the Bible. This has brought me such great happiness in my life and I'm sure this will continue for me even after this life. Eternity was never nearer to me than it is now.

> I love you, Adam

MONDAY, JUNE 30

After I had family home evening with Sam and his folks, he took me to the Visitor's Center on Temple Square. We spent a long time standing in front of the Christus statue. I turned to him and said, "You believe this too, right?"

And he goes, "No."

That worried me.

He turned to me and said, "I know it." That was good to hear.

It's getting so awkward at the door when he takes me home. I want him to kiss me but so far he hasn't. I guess it's because when we first met I told him I was practically engaged. Since I've never retracted that, he must think that's still the case. And he's not going to kiss someone who's engaged, and he's not even going to try to talk me out of it.

So where am I now with Mark? Nowhere. I don't even think about him much anymore. I guess all I was to him in NYC is a convenience. Not a necessity.

That's not what I want. I want the whole package. A husband, a mortgage, some kids, a temple wedding, and a father-in-law and a mother-in-law who love me.

I want to be the one that Sam's mom, on the phone, says, "Oh, I need to go. My daughter-in-law and her husband just came over."

It could be like that with Sam's folks. I'm sure it could.

I need to break up with Mark. And I will as soon as the exhibit opens. I'm too busy to do anything about that now.

WEDNESDAY

The exhibit opens tomorrow. Granny and I put in a twelve hour day. When we first got home, I showed her my new painting.

She goes, "Oh, my, yes! We've got to have that be the first thing people see when they enter the exhibit. Let's make that happen first thing in the morning."

We hugged and she told me how proud she was of me. I started to cry. But they were happy tears.

After Granny and I had something to eat, Sam came over and we went into our backyard. I asked him to teach me some church songs that families sing.

He taught me, "When the Family Gets Together."

We came in the house belting out the song. "That's a song for families, isn't it?" my mom asked. "So why are you two singing it?"

"Oh, no reason!" we both said too eagerly at the same time. And then we laughed.

Mom gave me the stare of death look.

"Let's go sing it for your mom and dad," I said.

And so we did.

After we left must have been when my dad called Mark and told him what was going on.

THURSDAY

The exhibit opened today with my painting! That made me happy.

It should have been a good day today because we had the opening of Granny's exhibit. And it would have been if Mark hadn't showed up and if Sam hadn't found out that Mark and I had been living together before I came out west.

What Sam said to me about that is the most hurtful thing anyone has ever said. "I don't want used merchandise." That's what he said.

Right now I'm sitting here waiting for my flight to Kennedy. I'm too numb to even cry.

Later-- I'm back in my apartment in NYC. I was dreading a big scene with Mark when I arrived at my apartment until I remembered he was out of town on business.

FRIDAY

Mark got back to NYC from his business trip. I told him he'd have to leave. He couldn't understand why. To tell the truth I was worried I'd change my mind but I didn't. But I might some day. But right now I just need some time to sort things out.

SATURDAY

I'm back to my old routine again. In some ways I like it. I like NYC. People going

places and doing things. People talk and
think faster. In whatever field you want, you
can find some of the best in the world there.

Sam keeps calling and I keep not
answering and deleting his messages. What a
jerk he turned out to be.

SUNDAY, JULY 6

It's early. Six am. I couldn't sleep. I have
a decision to make about church-- to go or
to give this whole thing up for good.

My first reaction is to just forget it. I
mean who needs it? There's lots of places I
can go and be told that basically I'm a tramp
without also being asked to donate ten
percent of my income.

Used merchandise? Is that what Sam
thinks I am? What a narrow-minded bigot!
Why didn't I pick up on that earlier?   Are
all Mormons that way?

Well, not all. Not Smith and Weston.
They're not for sure. When I told them about
Mark and me being intimate, they didn't
care because that was in my past and they

only care about what's in my future. They talked about repentance and forgiveness and hope.

So what do I do? What do I get rid of and what do I keep? That's what I can't decide. But I need to this morning.

I don't want used merchandise? What does that mean anyway? Does he think I'm like a used car? I'm a child of God. What kind of a jerk would say that?

So do I quit the church? That's what I want to do. And never think about it again. To just file it away in my mind and never bring it up again.

I could call Smith and Weston and see what they say. Only trouble is it's six thirty in the morning here so that would make it four thirty in the morning there. Too early.

I can probably predict what they'd tell me though. Keep the covenants I made when I was baptized. I could totally give it up now though. All I got to do is think about Sam telling me how great the church is. Oh, and that stupid thing he said in front of the Christus statue when I asked if he believed it and he said no, and then with this dramatic pause he goes, I know it's true.

Really, Sam? Do you also believe that people can be forgiven of their sins? Or isn't that in your take of what the church is about? To you I guess it's just for perfect people, like you, right? You big jerk!

Okay, to be fair, he didn't say I couldn't be forgiven. What he said is that he didn't want used merchandise. I guess as his wife, right? So tell me more, Utah. God can accept my repentance but you can't? Why's that? You have higher standards than God?

You know what? I wouldn't even want to be married to someone like that.

That's it. Because of Sam, I'm not going to church ever again. Who needs that anyway?

HALF AN HOUR LATER

Ok, I'm back. I just ate a quart of ice cream with nearly a container of chocolate syrup for breakfast. It was great!

About church-- I'm having second thoughts now about giving it up. Must have been the chocolate that got me out of the funk I was in.

I must believe in some of the church's teachings because once I arrived here I did throw Mark out of the apartment, which means I must believe that sex is reserved for marriage. And where did I learn that? It's one of the teachings of the church.

Also, I did bring my copy of the Book of Mormon with me. Why? Because of Third Nephi, beginning in Chapter 11 to the end of Third Nephi. There's no way that's not true. It's what Jesus would say if he visited the people in the New World after his resurrection.

And then there's Smith and Weston. I love them like they were my sisters. Probably more actually. Because if they were my sisters I'd have gotten mad at them for borrowing my stuff. I will always treasure the discussions we had and their patience and sense of humor and their faith and prayers. I love them with all my heart and I would never want to disappoint them.

And one more thing. I did feel the Spirit when I prayed and asked God if the Book of Mormon was true. I can't ever deny the feeling I had.

So what's the bottom line? It's this--I'm a member of the Church of Jesus Christ of Latter-Day Saints in NYC.

So now I need to get ready for church.
SUNDAY NIGHT

Somehow this morning I ended up in a Hispanic ward which at first I was disappointed about but actually turned out better than anything I could have ever imagined.

When I walked in, a woman my mom's age came over and gave me a hug and kissed me on the cheek. And that got me teary eyed.

Apparently she didn't speak much English because she took me over to someone about my age except with two adorable kids. This was Hermana Florez. Sister Flores spoke English and offered to translate for me.

So I sat with Sister Flores. Oh, her first name is Rebecca. I met her husband too. I can't remember his name but he seems nice. He's a helper to the bishop so he sat on the stand.

Rebecca Flores sat next to me and translated everything that anyone said. I helped her with her kids by drawing my elephant cartoons, which they loved.

I felt so welcomed and accepted. And it's impossible not to love them.

They're at church every week which in New York means they've turned down jobs with better pay just so they can keep the promises they made when they were baptized.

After sacrament meeting Rebecca Flores asked if I could teach one of their primary classes because their teacher hadn't come.

"You realize I don't speak Spanish, right?"

"Yes, just draw. They'll love that. Most of them speak English anyway. And if you want them to, they'll teach you some Spanish besides."

The kids and I had a great time. They were about ten years old and they taught me Spanish along the way. So, I'm thinking how many people in NYC know the Spanish word for elephant? Well, I do. It's elefante.

First we met as a class and then we went to a meeting with all the kids. And all I had to do was watch over my little class.

By the time church was over, each of the kids in my class gave me a hug. Of course I was in tears by that time. But they were tears of happiness.

Brother and Sister Flores offered me a ride home but I told them I'd just take the subway.

"Please come back and visit us," she said as I headed out the door.

"Could I come every Sunday?"

"Yes!. We would love to have you come!"

As I was leaving, one of the kids in my class came over to hug me. I knelt down so we'd be eye level and I held on to her as tears are running down my cheeks.

"Come next time," she said.

"I will. I promise."

And then I stood up, waved and hurried out the door.

When I got home, I went in my room and knelt down and thanked Father in Heaven for the blessing I'd received by going to church.

That's it, I thought. I'm in this for keeps.

Later that day, I called Smith and Weston. "Did you go to church today?" Weston asked.

"Si, gracias," I said. "Mucho bueno!"

And, the thing is, I totally meant it.

LATE TUESDAY AFTERNOON

Sam flew out here and showed up at my apartment. Mark was there too. He had been trying to charm me back into his life but I'd thrown him out. So they both ended up outside my door hoping to get in.

Sam gave it a shot through the door: "Charly, I forgive you. I probably would have done the same thing if I hadn't been a member of the church."

Can you believe that? The jerk calls me used merchandise and then flies out to tell me that he's forgiven me? I opened the door and then slammed it in his face.

He tried to amend his apology through the door but it only made me madder.

Finally I opened the door. "Why did you come here?"

"To apologize."

"You've done that. Now go."

I thought I'd gotten rid of him. But I hadn't. He followed me to my art class, made a fool of himself, got my teacher mad at me, and freaked out the model.

Just before I shut the door to the studio I told him that I was done with him. I told him to go home. So naturally I thought I'd got rid of him.

During the day Mark called and said he wanted to talk to me. I agreed to talk and told him to come over at eight.

At seven when I entered the apartment Mark was already there. He'd told Kevin at security that he'd forgotten his key.

Mark had brought a pizza and some wine. He talked about when we'd first met at Angelos and how much he was impressed with me.

He came close to convincing me of starting up again with him, but then I thought about the Primary class I'd taught on Sunday and how I couldn't let those girls down.

And then Sam comes busting through the door. He accuses Mark of being a New Yorker, which to Sam was the worst possible insult he could give.

Security came up and asked if Sam's supposed to be there. Mark says no and they start to drag him away and Sam calls out, "I had the wrong dream!"

And then with him holding onto the door frame while they're trying to pull him away, he goes on again about having the wrong dream. And then they drag him away.

So then there was just Mark and me. But I asked him to go.

And he does...for good.

As soon as Mark is gone, I call apartment security and tell them to let the police know it was okay that Sam was there. I didn't want Sam spending time in jail, as educational as an experience like that might be for him. They told me they'd take care of it.

So the police released Sam.

And that was it.

SUNDAY, SEPTEMBER 7

Thought I'd better write about what's happening. I've been so busy lately, doing too many things. I'm working on a children's illustrated book called "Elephants Can't Do That!" The idea came from being with Katie and Adam on my flight to Utah.

Also, a family bought the painting I did for Granny's exhibit. They've commissioned me to do two more. So after school and work, I paint until nine at night and then go home and get something to eat and go to bed.

I'm still attending the Hispanic ward and teaching Primary. One of our stake president's counselors who came to our ward today suggested I attend the YSA ward, whatever that is. I'm afraid they're going to make me leave the Hispanic Ward so I'm going to start learning Spanish just in case it's a requirement.

Several times a week I get something in the mail from Sam. Lots of long letters apologizing for what he'd said to me when he found out that Mark and I had been living together. At least now he knows what to apologize for.

I've read a few of them but mostly I just throw them in a drawer without reading them.

But even so, I can't help but compare Sam with guys I see in my classes. Like the guy who sits in front of me in my art history class. Always checking himself out, making sure he's still perfect. He uses a breath freshener every few minutes. Even when he's in class taking notes he tries to strike a heroic pose. And, what's worse, he only talks to those few he thinks are up to his level of distinction. I can't help but contrast that to Sam, before church, going to talk with a widow that he and his dad have home taught since Sam was fourteen. Sam's not perfect but at least he's better than Mister

"Look at me everybody!".
SUNDAY, NOVEMBER 9

The Primary did the sacrament program today. It was mucho bueno! They sang so well. They sounded great! I'm so proud of them!

The child's book is done so now I'm looking for a publisher. I'm nearly done with my third and last commissioned painting so I'm starting to come down from what really was a crazy schedule.

MONDAY

Today I got a package in the mail. I opened it and found a toy Ferris wheel, some left-over tickets from the first time we rode it the day we met each other. And what was more alarming, a paid round trip plane ticket in my name to SLC scheduled around Thanksgiving.

What is it with this guy? Why can't he take no for an answer?

In his letter he said the ticket was non-refundable so even if I didn't want to have anything to do with him I should use it anyway because it would give me an opportunity to spend Thanksgiving with my mom and dad and grandmother.

He said he had only two requirements for the tickets. One-- that I let him pick me up at the airport, and Two- that we go on the Ferris Wheel for at least ten minutes. That's all he would ever ask of me.

Oh, by the way, he goes, the tickets are non-refundable. "That means I can't get my money back if you decide not to come," he wrote.

Thank you, Sam, for explaining that to me. I never would have realized that non-refundable means no refund.

One thought about his offer. If I do go, it'd give me a break from the pace I'd been on, and, also I might be able to make it clear to Sam that I have no intention of ever being with him again. So I wrote back and told him I would accept his offer.

He'll think this will be good, but it won't. It will be very bad for him.

TUESDAY, NOVEMBER 25

Sam picked me up at the SLC airport. He had a sign just like before but I wasn't buying into us going back and reliving the past.

"I'm Utah, welcome to Sam," he said.

I scowled. "Yeah, right. Where'd you park the car?"

"Not far. Do you have anything else you need to get?"

"Just my mind. I must have lost it for agreeing to this," I grumbled.

"It's good to see you too," he said.

He drove us to the parking lot near the Ferris wheel.

"How long is this going to take?" I asked.

"Not long."

Somehow he'd talked Mr. Raferty into being there.

"This is Charly," he said, "We just got engaged and you're the first person we've told."

"Congratulations again, you two."

We got in and Mr. Raferty started the Ferris wheel. I looked at my watch. "You've got ten minutes."

"First I want to apologize again for what I said to you when I found out about you and Mark."

"You mean when you said you didn't want used merchandise?" I asked.

He winced. "Yes. I'm so sorry. That was a terrible thing to say. You must have felt awful."

"Yes, I did as a matter of fact."

"It was cruel of me. I mean you'd already gone through the repentance process."

"Exactly. I was totally forgiven by God, but not by you. That's because you have higher standards than God, right?"

"I should have been more charitable and kind."

"That's right. You should have. What you said made me feel like you thought I sleep with any random guy who comes along. And even if that was true, I still wouldn't be used merchandise."

"No, of course not. You're a daughter of God and He loves you."

"That's right. I am. And the atonement is infinite and eternal."

He sighed. "Yeah, it is. I'm so sorry."

I was puzzled by whatever tactic he was using here. It wasn't what most guys do. You know where the guy goes "I said I was wrong so let's just forget it and move on." Or my all time favorite guy apology: "I'm sorry you misunderstood what I said." Every guy I've ever known does one of those two and says it was an apology. So why isn't Sam doing that?

"You said you didn't want used merchandise! How could you say that to anyone? You made it sound like this was a part time job for me. Well, it wasn't. "

"Of course not. You had feelings for Mark and I'm sure he did for you."

"That's true. We did." I sighed. "Oh, for your information, I'm done with Mark now."

"How come?"

"I teach a Primary class in a Hispanic ward and I've got to show the girls and boys in my class the right example."

"Good for you for serving in the church."

"Well, it's certainly not because of your pathetic example."

"I understand."

"Sam, let me tell you something. To Father in Heaven I'm not a list of the mistakes I made. Because of Jesus Christ I've been forgiven for whatever sins I've committed. What you said was the most cruel thing anyone has ever said to me and I don't think I will ever be able to forgive you for what you said to me."

He nodded. "More than anything I wish I hadn't said it. I am so sorry."

I kept bringing up all the things I'd felt and he kept agreeing with me about what a jerk he'd been until finally I'd said it all. It was all out in the open.

"That's it. I'm done. Let's let Mr. Raferty get back to his family," I said.

"Okay." Sam told Mr. Raferty that we were done.

As we left, I gave Mr. Raferty a hug and thanked him for doing this for us. Sam shook his hand.

"So, now what?" he asked as we walked to his car.

"What did you have in mind?"

"To ask you to marry me."

"Yeah, right," I grumbled.

"I'm serious."

I stopped walking. "Are you out of your mind? You have the worst sense of timing of anyone I have ever known!"

"Why can't we at least talk about it?" he asked.

"Look, you can't go from me telling you what a jerk you've been to talking about us getting married."

"We wouldn't get married right away. I'm suggesting we get married in the temple. The earliest that could happen is one year from your baptismal date. So that's like seven months. You'll have lots of time to consider the idea." He paused. "Just think about it. That's all I'm asking."

"I don't want to think about it! I want to go home, see my mom and dad, exercise, take a shower, talk to Granny, watch football games and eat junk food! I certainly do not want to plan some stupid wedding with you for god's sake!" I shook my head. "Sorry. I've been working hard not to take the name of the Lord God in vain, but once in a while it creeps out, mostly when I'm out-of-my-mind angry at someone like I am now at you."

"I understand."

I paused. "What temple were you thinking of?"

"The Salt Lake Temple."

I threw my hands up in the air. "See, there you go again! That is so like you! Why not the Washington DC Temple?"

"Because this is closer."

"To you, yeah, but what about my family?"

"Actually, your mom and dad and grandmother live in Utah now."

"You think I don't know that? Sam, I swear, you're making me crazy! Quit with the temple wedding talk."

"Okay."

We stood there looking at each other.

I felt a little bad for dumping on him so much. He had tried so hard to apologize. That's not easy for a guy.

I sighed. "Could you perhaps give me like a quick hug to welcome me home?" I asked in my little girl voice.

"I can do that."

We held each other tight. "That feels so good," he said.

"Yeah, I got to admit it does." I cleared my throat. "What would you think about kissing me?" I asked.

"I'd be okay with that." He started to make his move.

I got mad at him. "Not here, okay?"

"Where?"

"I don't know! Don't make me stage this for you!"

"What does that mean?"

"Oh, I can't believe you sometimes. Look, just forget it, ok? Take me home. I'm tired and I want to get some sleep. I had to wake up at four thirty this morning to make my flight."

So he drove me home. And we didn't talk.

When he pulled into our driveway and got out to get my bag from the trunk, I figured I'd probably never see him again. And, strangely enough, that made me sad.

He opened the door for me. I got out and said, "Okay, you can kiss me now."

"What?"

"Kiss me now."

"Here?"

"Yes."

"Your mom and dad are looking out the window at us."

"I don't care!"

Granny opened the door and started down the stairs. My mom and dad were right behind her.

"Look who's home for Thanksgiving!" Granny called out as she and my folks came toward us.

"What are you waiting for?" I complained to Sam.

"You want me to kiss you now?" he asked.

"Yes, hurry!"

"Okay."

"Welcome home!" Granny said, about to hug me.

"Later, okay?" I said to Granny.

Granny stopped.

Sam also. "Later for me?"

"No, you go ahead but hurry."

So Sam kissed me.

It was actually a slightly longer kiss than either of us had anticipated.

"We'll wait until you two are...uh...done," Granny said. "We'll be in the house."

Granny shooed my folks inside.

So we were alone again.

We were both embarrassed. "Well, that was...uh, okay," I said, doing my best to minimize the effect it had had on me.

"Yeah it was," he goes. "More than okay really. It was more like amazing."

"I wouldn't go that far. But it was...uh...certainly...above industry standards I would say."

"What are you talking about?"

I shrugged. "I have no idea."

"Is it okay for me to tell you that I love you?" he asked.

I shrugged my shoulders. "Not yet but wouldn't it be crazy if we ended up deciding some day that we actually love each other?"

"I never stopped loving you."

"I did. I stopped big time."

"Of course. You had every reason to do that."

"That's true. I did. "

I needed to go. "Will I see you again before I head back to New York?" I asked, suddenly feeling vulnerable.

"You will. As much as you want."

"What time do you get up in the morning?" I asked.

"Anytime you want me to."

"Maybe we could go fishing," I said.

"Fishing season is over."

That set me off. "I don't care, okay? I just want to be with you!" I stopped and shook my head. "Sorry. I may have actually over-stated that."

"I love you."

"Are you sure?"

"Yeah, I'm sure," he said.

"Well, we'll see how it goes. If the time ever comes when I see you and don't want to tell you what a jerk you are, I think we'll be almost there."

"Fair enough," he said. "Why did you ask me to kiss you?"

I started to blush. "That's a very good question. The truth? This is a little embarrassing to say but I wanted to see what it would be like." I sighed. "I guess that shows how shallow and immature I am, doesn't it?"

"Not really. How was it?"

I shrugged. "It was okay I guess."

He seemed disappointed. "Just okay?"

"Oh, give me a break! What is it with guys anyway?"

He smiled. "You're right."

"I've got to go. Maybe with time the friendship we had will come back."

"Maybe so. We'll just have to see how it goes. Well, I'll go now."

He helped me carry my luggage to the front steps and then left.

Once home, my dad and Granny and I settled into a familiar routine-- watching football. Even during the fourth quarter with the game tied, and my dad and Granny giving suggestions to the team, and my mom in the kitchen making something to eat for us that we'd take for granted, I found myself wondering if I would ever want to be married to Sam.

Don't know. Not sure if I ever will know.

WEDNESDAY

Sam picked me up at nine. He drove me to the Visitor's Center on Temple Square and we walked around.

And then we drove back to his house and we talked with his mom and dad.

When I was alone with his mom, I asked, "When Sam apologized to me, it was different than when he apologized when he came to visit me in New York. Do you know what his apology was then?"

"Yes, he said that he told you that he forgave you. That he probably would have done the same thing if he hadn't been a member of the Church."

"In Utah he gave me worst insult I've ever received and then he flies out to tell me that he forgives me. I couldn't believe it."

"When he came back and told me what he'd said, I told him where he'd gone wrong. He asked me to help him know what to say if he ever got a chance to apologize again. We've been working on it. How'd he do this time?"

"Much better."

"I hope you're not mad at me for trying to help him," she said.

"No." I paused. "Actually, I'm flattered that you wanted us to get back together again."

"Can I tell you something? You're the best thing that has ever happened to Sam," she said.

I was surprised she'd say that. "In what way?"

"Don't tell him this, but in the past I've often thought, but of course have never said to him, that Sam would have made a good Pharisee. He lives the letter of the law but sometimes forgets the spirit of the law-- to be charitable and kind to others. The Savior is our example for that. Sometimes Sam forgets that."

"I've seen that in him too," I said.

"Yes, I know. I was so disappointed when he told me what he'd said to you."

"You mean about not wanting used merchandise?" I asked.

"Yes. What an awful thing to say." She sighed. "I'm so sorry he said that to you. Please forgive him."

"I'm working on that."

"I think Sam would be a better follower of the teachings of Jesus Christ with you as his wife than with anyone else I can think of."

I was surprised but pleased she'd say that.

"That's what I want to be." I said and then added for clarification. "I mean a disciple of Jesus Christ."

"I can see that in you. Whenever you meet someone, you light up. You look for what's wonderful in that person. Not everyone does that, you know."

"Thank you for saying that. It means a lot to me."

Sam and I spent the rest of the day at his folks' home. I helped him clean the garage. I think we were both relieved not having to talk about any future we might have together.

In the afternoon Sam offered to help me do some family history.

"Why would I want to do that?" I asked.

"So you can be baptized in the temple for your ancestors who've died."

At first I wasn't that excited but by the end of the day, with Granny's knowledge of her parents and grandparents, we had temple slips for my great grandmother and great grandfather and two aunts I'd never known who'd died in their teens.

"Maybe in December when you come back here for Christmas you can be baptized for these relatives of yours. You'll need a temple recommend for baptisms from your bishop though."

"I'll get one. Why are you doing this?" I asked.

"My goal is to win over your family one generation at a time."

Okay, I got to say it. Good move, Sam.

SATURDAY, November 29

I'm on my flight back to NYC. Things have definitely changed in the last few days. Sam and I are at least talking again.

SUNDAY, DECEMBER 21

Even though I'd like to, I'm not going home for Christmas. I have two commissioned paintings I have to get done and delivered before Christmas. I finished the last one yesterday so on Monday I'm driving to Vermont where they're spending Christmas so my paintings can be given as Christmas presents. Oh, and also, of course, to collect my check.

TUESDAY

Back from Vermont. Stayed in a great hotel in the woods. Beautiful place. Took lots of pictures.

I'm happy to have some extra money. Last night I called Granny and told her about my success. She welcomed me into the select group of artists who actually make money for their work.

Tonight Rebecca Flores called and invited me to their house for Christmas. I told her she didn't need to do that, that I'd be okay by myself. She said their Christmas would be much better with me there with

them, and, besides, her kids wanted me to
come.

I know you're supposed to turn down
invitations like that because it makes you
appear needful. But, the truth is, for the first
time in my life I'll be all alone for
Christmas, and so, basically, I am needful.
So I said yes.

CHRISTMAS DAY

I'm back from being with Rebecca and
her family! What a wonderful day! And my
Spanish is coming along. I understood about
half of what Rebecca's mom said

I love that family!

I hope I'll be like Rebecca and always
remember those around me who are alone on
Christmas.

DECEMBER 26

Sam called and told me he wanted to
come out and see me. "I can't stand to be
away from you any longer."

"That's the way I feel too."

"If you came, where would you stay?" I asked. "You can't stay with me."

"I know. A hotel I guess."

"That would cost a lot of money."

"I don't care."

"How about if I come to see you?" I asked.

A long pause. "Would you do that?"

"Yeah I would...for you. And I just sold some paintings so I have a little extra money."

"Please come then. I'm going crazy here."

So I got off the phone and booked my ticket for the next day.

MONDAY, DECEMBER 29

I'm here at home in SLC in my room writing this after spending a day with Sam. He took me cross-country skiing. It was not something I would have thought of doing myself. Like "Hey, everyone, it's freezing cold in the mountains and they're full of snow! We could all freeze to death if we even ventured into that environment. I know! Let's all strap sticks on our feet and trudge through the woods! Who knows? If we're lucky, we might not even die!"

Like everything associated with Sam, it also had its charms. And in the end I was thinking, "Winter, what a great time of year!"

TUESDAY

Sam and I went to the temple and I was baptized for my great grandmother and two great aunts I'd never known.

Sam baptized me for them. I was so happy to be doing this for them. After that we went to the Visitors Center at Temple Square.

Sam and I had dinner with my folks and Granny. After dinner we went through each other's family photo albums (first at our home and then over at Sam's place) so we could see the other grow up from page to page

I'm not sure what Sam was thinking as we looked at these family photos, but I hoped that someday I'd have a son who looked like Sam had as a child. He was such an appealing kid! In addition, I learned much that reflects well on Sam..

He was a Boy Scout and earned his Eagle rank, which apparently is a big deal.

Sam served a mission in Minnesota. I saw photos of him with people about to be baptized. He loves to talk about these people he grew to love and still loves. When I contrast that kind of concern with any other guy I've ever known, Sam comes out looking very good.

The next day Sam came shopping at a mall with me for a pair of shoes. In a way it was my little test because guys as a rule don't like to go shopping with a woman.

We must have gone to ten stores.

"Sorry this is taking so long," I said.

"It doesn't matter. I'm with you. That's all that counts."

"You must really like me."

"I do." He reached for my hand. It was

great holding hands with him. I didn't see any other couples holding hands.

I love it when we look into each other's eyes or when he gives me a big smile.

Or when I got him to play along with me when we met up at the front of a store where we'd separated for a few minutes.

"Excuse me, my name is Katrina. I'm a figure skater for the Rumanian Olympic team. I have decided to denounce my citizenship and stay in America, but the Rumanian authorities are trying to stop me. I need you to drive me to a small village in Idaho where I will be safe."

He looked at me and then gave me a big smile. "I will take you wherever you want, no matter what danger there might be."

"Really? That's very kind of you."

"That's the kind of guy I am."

We played the game for ten minutes, me telling him I'd seen one of the bad guys and we needed to hurry.

It ended with us putting on winter

coats with parkas which we were going to use to walk past the bad guys.

In the end we were both laughing so hard people were staring at us, so we quit our game and left the store.

"It's always fun with you," I said.

"For me too. Without you my life would be so boring."

"That means we're good for each other," I said.

"Yes, I agree."

I love his smile. I love when I can get him to laugh.

WEDNESDAY, NEW YEAR'S EVE

Tonight we went to the dance at the church. We kissed at midnight. What a great tradition!

NEW YEAR'S DAY

Sam and I watched football with my folks and Granny. And of course we ate. I've had enough nachos and celery filled with cream cheese to last a year.

JANUARY 2

I flew back to NYC.

Bottom line from the trip? I'm in love. We're even talking about getting married.

MONDAY, JANUARY 5

After class today Dr. D told me my work has improved dramatically. He asked me why.

I told him about Granny's advice to pick a theme you feel so strongly about that you're sure you could never express it on canvas—and then do it. I also told him about recently becoming a Mormon. He shook his head. "I don't see how that could possibly make any difference."

"I know you don't but you should find out for yourself what I'm talking about."

He sighed. "Life is complicated enough as it is without throwing religion into the mix."

"What it has done for me is to make life better."

"Well, then I'm glad for you. I just know that's not for me."   He then walked to the next person in the class.

The next day I gave him a copy of the Book of Mormon. He said he would probably never read it but said he would put it in his library at home and thanked me for it.

He's right though about my work. It has reached a new level. Life is too important to waste it on random bowls of fruit. Every person I meet is a child of God. That makes everyone a treasure just waiting to be discovered as I get to know them.

Adam, look around you each day. Every person you see was once with you in the pre-existence before the world was created. Each one is a son or daughter of Father in Heaven, just as you are. Nobody is common or ordinary. They are all worth your respect and consideration. This is what I've learned from the Plan of Happiness. Be kind to the people you see each day.

This is what I've tried to do since being baptized. I hope you will do that too.

Love,
Mom

SUNDAY, FEBRUARY 1

Today after church Sam called and said he can't stand not being with me. He wants to come visit me around Valentine's Day.

"Are you serious? That would be impresionante!"

"Excuse me?" Sam asked.

"That's the Spanish word for awesome!"

"I'm glad you like the idea."

"What about your classes? Also, can we afford it? This doesn't mean we won't have a honeymoon, does it?"

"No, it doesn't mean that. Can you find me a place to stay?"

"Yeah, I think so. My friend in the Spanish Ward might be able to put you up. She's married and has two amazing kids. She once told me they have an extra room so maybe you could stay there. How's your Spanish, Compadre?"

"Uh...bueno...mucho bueno?"

I laughed. "Wow, I can't believe it! You speak like a native!"

"I've often been told that. What can I say? It's a gift."

"Yes, a gift for self-deception, that's what it is, my friend. Same as me in my Primary class. The kids in my class are laughing all the time but I'm not even trying to be funny."

I was so happy that day knowing that Sam is coming to see me. I have so many places I want to take him. But, also, just to be with him will be so great!

I'm so pumped!

WEDNESDAY, FEBRUARY 18

I'm feeling a little better today.

Sam left yesterday. Too bad I got the flu while he was here. But we had two amazing days though before I got sick. He took me to dinner on Valentine's Day and we went to a Broadway play. I got the tickets at half price. (I know a guy.)

Tuesday morning he sat with me while I slept on the couch between times I had to run to the bathroom to hurl. Once though, I didn't make it.

He cleaned it up.

"I'm so sorry."

"Don't worry about it."

It was eleven in the morning and his flight wasn't until seven at night.

"Sam, look, you don't need to be here. I'm just going to sleep anyway. Is there some

place you'd like to visit before you head
back home?"

He paused, so I knew he did have such
a place in mind.

"You've got five hours before you need
to catch a taxi for Kennedy. Where would
you like to go?"

"Well, I have thought about going to the
Museum of Natural History sometime."

"Go then! I'll take a nap. Come back in
four hours and wake me up."

"Are you sure?"

"Of course. This can't be much fun for
you."

Eventually I talked him into it.

At first I was okay after he left. I tried
to imagine him having a great time at the
museum, and be pleased that I'd given him
that option, but then, also I began to wonder
how he could leave me when I was sick. I
began to wonder if he really loved me that
much.

I forced myself into getting up and taking a shower and doing my hair so he'd see me looking good before he left. But I was so weak it was hard to do even the most simple things.

At some point, after I finished, I looked into the mirror and realized I still looked sick.

I remember looking at the clock and thinking he still had three hours before he was due to come back, and by that time I'll be weaker and look even worse and that he'll take one look at me and dump me all over again because he didn't really love me that much. How could he love me if he was willing to spend his last hours here in NYC at some stupid science museum instead of with me?

And then there was a knock at the door.

I went to the door and looked through the security port and saw that it was Sam. I opened the door. "I didn't expect you back so soon."

"I'd been at the museum for half an hour and I thought to myself, 'What am I doing here looking at dinosaur bones when the only thing I really care about in this town is Charly. I need to be with her."

That got to me big time. "Thank you."

He came in and held me in his arms.

"You shouldn't be doing this," I said. "I'll only make you sick."

"I don't care. You okay?"

I told him how I'd felt shortly after he left, ending with, "You tossed me aside once. I'm afraid I'll go our entire married life worrying that you're going to get tired of me some day and decide I'm not worth the effort, so maybe it isn't that great of an idea for us to get married."

"Are you out of your mind?" he asked with what he thought was a New York accent, but it was so bad it made me snicker.

"We need to talk," he said, borrowing an expression I'd used on him.

We went to the couch and sat down.

And talked.

At first he couldn't understand why I'd encouraged him to go visit the museum but then ended up feeling abandoned because he'd done what I'd suggested.

It wasn't easy to explain. I told him that probably I'd have been okay if he hadn't already dumped me when he found out about Mark and me.

"My fear is that sometime, even after we're married, you'll find another reason to leave me. I didn't know I'd feel abandoned again until after you left for the museum. I'm worried this may keep coming up again and again even after we're married."

"I will never leave you, no matter what," he said.

"How can you say that?"

"I come from a long line of men who stayed with their wives," he said.

"Good for you," I said bitterly. "I wish I could say the same."

"What are you talking about?"

"My dad left my mom for another woman when I was ten years old. He was only gone like a week before he came to his senses and returned. Because he'd hurt my mom so much, he and I have never got along much after that. I know I should forgive him but, truth is, I haven't yet."

"Sorry you and your mom had to go through that."

"It's just life, right? Sooner or later everyone is disappointed by the people they love."

"I hope you're never disappointed in me," he said, reaching for my hand. And then he sighed. "I mean never disappointed in me again...in the future..after we're married."

"I know what you mean." I looked down at our entwined hands. "Germs."

"They're your germs, so it's okay."

I smiled. "Tell me that when you're hurling your guts out in the plane restroom."

"Whatever price I have to pay for holding your hand, it's worth it."

I smiled. "That is so cheesy."

"It's the truth though."

"Okay, but don't say I didn't warn you."

He seemed content to just be with me. I guess I was content too because I fell asleep.

I woke up about half an hour later. And he was still there.

I looked at the clock. "We don't have much time left before you need to go."

"If you want, I can stay another day."

"No, I'll be fine. I'm starting to feel better anyway. Thank you though."

"Let me ask you a question," he said. "Are you still okay with, if we do get married, we do it in the temple?"

"Yeah, sure, why do you ask?"

"What about your mom and dad? They won't be there to see their only child get married."

"My mom knows this is important to me. She'll be okay with it."

"What about your dad?"

I pursed my lips. "I know this isn't very charitable but I don't really care what he thinks."

He nodded his head "I can understand why you'd feel that way."

He didn't say anything after that.

"But what?" I asked after a minute or two.

"Do you ever hope that someday your mom and dad get baptized? So they can go to the temple and be sealed for time and eternity like we will?"

I shook my head. "He doesn't deserve that."

"And he never will?"

I shook my head. "I know where this is going. Your point is how can I accept the fact that I've been forgiven of my sins but not be willing to want my dad's sins forgiven? Right?"

"Something like that."

"I know I should forgive him but so far I can't."

"I understand. Maybe with time, though, right?"

"Maybe." I looked at the clock. "You'd better go now if you're going to make your flight."

"You're mad at me, aren't you?" he asked.

"A little. It's so easy to tell someone who's been hurt to forgive the person who did the damage. But when it's something that happened in your life, it's harder to do that."

"I understand."

"With all due respect, I doubt if that's true." I stood up. "Look, you've got to go. If you miss your flight and I have to put up with you for another day..." I smiled. "That would be absolutely great...but let's go with Plan A for now."

"Are you mad at me?"

"No, not really. It's good for us to talk about things like this...you know...difficult issues we're both still dealing with. Do you have any I should know about?"

He stopped to think about it. "I think I've taken care of everything."

"Good for you." I looked at the clock. "You'd better go before the traffic gets impossible."

He grabbed his luggage and we walked to the door. He set it down and then moved in to kiss me.

I put my finger on his lips. "Not on my lips. Kiss my cheek. There's less germs there."

He kissed me on the cheek and then shook his head. "Sorry but this isn't working for me," he said.

I shrugged. "Okay, go ahead, get sick, see if I care."

He kissed me on the lips. It was good but I was still worried he'd get sick. So eventually I pulled away. "Get out of here, I need to get some sleep."

I hugged him again, "Thank you for being so good to me."

"That comes easy when you're in love. I'll call you when I get home."

"You'd better. Oh, if you ever get sick after we're married, I'll take care of you too."

"It's a deal." He smiled went out into the hall and then turned and headed for the elevator.

I went to the window and watched him hail a cab. I was impressed the way he did it. He didn't look like a rooky anymore.

SUNDAY, MARCH 22

I've been so busy lately I've neglected writing in here.

Right after Sam left me in February I was told that three graduating seniors would be honored to have an exhibit on graduation week. The only problem was I needed to have ten paintings done by that time.

So between class projects that's all I've been doing.

I feel awful that I haven't been able to spend more time with Sam. We talk every night but sometimes I'm so exhausted I fall asleep on the phone.

I'm doing good though. I've finished seven of the ten I need. Well, actually, I'm not using one of them, so I've still got four more to go.

SUNDAY, APRIL 19

I've finished all ten paintings! Tomorrow the committee will choose the top three artists. Here's hoping.

MONDAY

I was chosen! I'm so excited!

All I want from my life now is to sleep and not do anything for a few days.

TUESDAY

Sam and his folks drove out for my graduation, which is tomorrow. My mom and dad and Granny flew out.

WEDNESDAY, APRIL 22

I graduated! Happy day!

THURSDAY

Sam asked me if this would be a good day for him to propose to me.

"Propose what?" I asked.

'You know. Marriage."

"Yeah, I know. I get to pick the place though, okay?"

He agreed.

A part of me wanted to embarrass him like asking him to propose on a crowded subway but in the end I decided against that because by then I'd forgiven him and I knew that he loved me and that I didn't need to punish him anymore.

So I asked him to propose to me in a wooded area of Central Park.

Even wooded areas in Central Park got lots of people. So about a hundred looked on as he got down on his knees and proposed.

I love New Yorkers! They all cheered when I said yes and we kissed.

SUNDAY, JULY 12

We were married on Wednesday July 8 in the Salt Lake Temple while my mom and dad and Granny sat in a waiting room for us to be finished and come out for pictures.

We had a reception that night at the church, spent our first night together in a hotel in Provo, and then drove the next morning to St. George.

Sam had planned for us to go on a big hike early the next morning but I ruined any plans he had for that. Actually, though, he didn't complain.

SUNDAY, AUGUST 15

We've been staying in the basement of Sam's folks' place, but tomorrow we're moving to Provo so Sam can finish up his senior year. He just has one more semester. We'll stay with his aunt in Provo until we find a place to stay.

MONDAY

I flew to NYC to sign contracts for my children's book "Elephants Can't Do That!" We still haven't found an apartment but Sam will be looking while I'm gone.

SUNDAY, SEPTEMBER 20

Time to get caught up in this.

I was in New York when Sam picked out our apartment. He closed the deal without me seeing the place He was so proud of how cheap it was.

One problem. When he looked at the apartment, he didn't ask where the shower was. Not until we moved in did we find out it's in the kitchen. Yes, the kitchen! Of course there's a shower curtain but we have to hook it up each time we take a shower. And of course when you step out of the shower and dry off, it's awkward to be doing it in a kitchen.

There are times when you want privacy. For me the shower experience is one of those times.

Our landlord and his wife have four boys: 10, 12,14,and 16. They'll know when one of us is taking a shower because they'll be able to hear when water is running for a shower. I think it might be possible for them to crawl to the window well and, even though there's a shower curtain, they might still be able to see me drying myself. So I had Sam make some cardboard inserts we can tape over our kitchen window. That seems to work okay.

My dad used to complain I took such long showers. This has totally cured me of that.

But other than that, the apartment is okay I guess. It's true we can hear the boys upstairs rough-housing and they play their video games so loud it gives us headaches.

SUNDAY, SEPTEMBER 27

On Wednesday my mom and dad made an unannounced visit while Sam was taking a shower...in the kitchen.

When I went to the door and saw that it was my mom and dad. It made me smile.

"Mom and Dad, what a surprise! Come in and let me show you around, especially our kitchen!" I practically yelled it so Sam could hear me.

He turned off the water, grabbed a towel and ran into the bedroom and shut the door before they could see him.

"You wouldn't believe what a good deal we got for this place!" I said enthusiastically. "This is our hallway," I said taking my folks on a tour. I next pointed to the square structure in the middle of our apartment. "And this is the furnace room. It also contains the hot water heater for the house."

"And this is our living room!" They saw a cheap plastic couch with duct tape over one of the torn cushions.

I led them a couple more feet to an easel holding a painting I was working on. "And this is my studio."

I glimpsed as Sam, wearing jeans and a sweatshirt, but still barefoot, ran for the kitchen. A minute later I could hear him mopping the floor which needed to be done whenever we took a shower.

A few minutes later Sam opened the kitchen door and came in to greet my folks. He was wearing an old fishing hat, but I could see some shampoo sticking out the back of his hat.

"Look, Sam, it's mom and dad! I'm giving them a tour of our apartment! Why don't you show them our kitchen?"

"Oh, yea, sure, watch your step. I was just mopping the floor."

"I'm very impressed you're helping out," my mom said.

"Oh, yes."

"Sam washes the floor almost every day," I said with a huge grin directed at him.

We entered the kitchen. Sam had put things back the way we had it after a shower. The shower curtain folded up and put in a drawer, two baby booties over the hot and cold water faucets, a pot of plastic flowers hanging from the shower spout. He'd done it all.

"What a compact kitchen!" my mom said. "No wasted steps to get things here."

"No, none."

I was enjoying this way too much.

My dad hit his head on one of the hot air ducts as we entered our bedroom. We went into the living room and sat down. Sam and me in kitchen chairs, my mom and dad on the sofa.

The boys upstairs started wrestling and we couldn't carry on a conversation. We were all just staring at the ceiling. They broke a lamp or something. Their dad came in from outside and yelled at them, then it was quiet, and he left. And then one of the boys started to practice his trombone.

My mom was almost in tears as she realized where her daughter was living.

Mom asked what it was they smelled, and I said beans. My dad says he likes beans. So I invited them to stay for dinner. What else could I do?

So they stayed,. We were having beans using a ham bone for the sixth straight time. The same ham bone for several batches of beans was Sam's idea. So basically it was beans with no taste.

My mom, in trying to admire the baby booties on the wall, touched it and water started dripping onto the table.

So we had to admit that this was also where we took showers.

My dad lost it and said this was unacceptable and that we should let him pay the difference each month for an adequate apartment. He said he'd set up a joint account and we could pay him back after Sam graduated and got a job.

Sam said. "We don't need your money."

And my dad said, "She's my daughter. And what is this slop we're eating here? I don't want her getting sick because she's not eating right."

And Sam adds, "We're doing all right, but even if we weren't, we wouldn't take a dime from you."

So they left.

Sam was so mad he wouldn't speak to me.

We avoided each other until it was time for bed.

I got ready for bed, putting on my most frumpy sleep attire-sweat pants and a hoodie.

Sam was studying. I sat down beside him.

He didn't even look up.

"Sam, we need to talk."

He looked up and glared at me. "So, talk."

"We can't go to bed mad."

"Why not?"

"Our bed's too small for us to get far enough away from each other. We need to resolve this."

"You set me up for what happened."

I took a deep breath. "Okay, tell me why you think I set you up."

"When you saw your mom and dad at the door, you could have told me they were here before you even opened the door, so I didn't have to make a mad dash to the bedroom."

"You're right. I should have done that."

"And why did you invite them to stay for dinner? You knew what they'd think about what we were eating."

I nodded. "Okay, you're right. I shouldn't have asked them for dinner. What else?"

"All the time they were here you were smirking at me, like you were paying me back for putting you in such a ghetto apartment."

"Was I really smirking?"

"You were."

I sighed. "Maybe I was. Truth is I was enjoying seeing you squirm when they discovered all the bad things about this place."

"I expected better of you, Charly."

"You're right. I did mess up and for that I apologize."

He hugged me. "Now can we go to bed?" he asked hopefully.

"Not yet. I have a few things I need to tell you."

"Okay."

"In the first place, I can see now that I should have never agreed for us to stay in this apartment. Even though you'd put down a down payment, when I saw it, I should have said, this dump is totally unacceptable so we'll have to find something else."

"You hated it that much the first time you saw it?"

"I did."

"Why didn't you say something then?"

"Because I wanted to be the dutiful wife, the non-complaining mousey spousey. We had such a great honeymoon. I didn't want to get in the way of that. I should have said, 'Sam, there's no way I'm living here. We need to get our deposit back and go find another apartment.' But I didn't do that. Well, rest assured, from now on I'm never going to agree to anything just to avoid a disagreement. And you should never do that for me either. Let's just be totally honest with each other, all the time, in every situation, no matter what. Agreed?"

He sighed. "Agreed. I shouldn't have put a deposit down on an apartment you hadn't seen."

"That's right. So from now on we'll always be up front with each other. Okay?"

"Agreed. Have we made up?"

"I think so."

"So does that mean good times are coming?" he asked with a silly grin on his face.

"Just around the corner, my boy, just around the corner."

"I'll get ready," he said, heading for the bathroom.

"Wait. One thing more if I may," I said.

He stopped in his tracks and turned around. "Yes?"

"Lose the aftershave, okay? I'm sure you like it but it's not working for me. It's like making love to a medicine cabinet."

"Okay, good to know."

So with all those issues resolved, we went to bed and had a good time.

I love being married!

Adam,

When I first started using this as a diary, I never imagined that someday my son in his twenties would be reading this. But if this works out the way I hope it does, by the time you read this, you'll be married, so hopefully you won't freak out to know your birth mom and dad enjoyed intimacy as a married couple. Even when times were bad and we had no money and our car quit working, this was one area of our life where we could forget our troubles.

Love,
Mom

SUNDAY, OCTOBER 18

I've got some time today to get caught up on this. Can't believe it's been so long since I last wrote in here.

We've both been busy. Sam and I are both working. He works early mornings doing custodial work on campus. I work in the art supplies section of the bookstore. Two days a week I'm there until closing so I don't get home until a little after nine. He has to go to bed at least by nine in order to get up at 3 am for work. So we don't see very much of each other. My Elephants book is completely done and scheduled for publication so I don't need to worry about it anymore.

We're busy during the week. Weekends are good though, especially after church. That's our time together.

SUNDAY, NOVEMBER 8

Scratch the part about Sundays being good. Sam has been called to be a ward clerk in our campus ward so he has meetings starting at 7 in the morning and doesn't get back home until two hours after our ward gets out. I miss not having more time with him but at least I know he's serving God.

The trouble with being in a young marrieds ward is almost every Sunday I find out who else is now pregnant. No such news for Sam and me though. It's not because we're not trying.

I'm thinking I should talk to Sam about us getting both checked out by a doctor. But I'm a little reluctant to bring it up because I'm afraid it will hurt his ego. Guys are so weird.

Sometimes I feel like life is taking us away from each other, and that we're not as close as we were when we first got married. I hate it that it might be true but I'm not sure what to do about it.

The problem with me talking about the fact that I'm not getting pregnant is that he'll think I'm blaming him and then he'll get defensive and that will end the conversation, with me feeling like the bad guy. (How come there are never any bad girls in discussions like this? Oh, wait, that's obvious, isn't it?)

DECEMBER 7   Not pregnant.

JANUARY 3   Not pregnant.

FEBRUARY 7   Not pregnant

MARCH 7   Not pregnant

APRIL 11   Not pregnant

April 18

Today when Sam came home from his meetings, he found me asleep on the couch with a bunch of crumpled tissues scattered around me.

He sat down next to me and that woke me up. "You okay?"

I shook my head. "Yeah, sure."

"What's with the tissues?"

"Allergies."

"C'mon, Charly, tell me what's going on?":

"I found out in church today that Clarissa, Megan, and Ann Marie are expecting."

"So?"

"So why aren't I pregnant?"

"I don't know. Maybe you should go see a doctor and find out what he says."

"I'm not the only player in this game you know. Maybe we should both go to a doctor."

"You think this is my fault?" he asked.

"Don't do the 'I am a manly man' bit on me, Sam. Why can't we look at this as something we both need to work on?"

His shoulders slumped. "You're right. It's probably me."

"Did I say that? No, I did not. We're in this together, okay? Let's just find out where we stand on this, and then do something to make it better."

He let out a big sigh and then said, "You're right. We need to work on this."

We talked a lot that afternoon. He told me that sometimes lately he dreaded us being intimate because for him this was starting to be like another mid-term exam, which he would fail once again and give him another reason to feel inadequate.

I had no idea he felt that kind of pressure. I guess being a guy is harder than it looks.

Anyway, we're going to try to concentrate on spending as much quality time together so we can confide in each other what worries us the most.

I told him that my greatest fear is loving kids so much but never being able to have any. He talked about how hard it would be for him to never have a son or daughter he could take fishing.

We'll go together to see a doctor so we can know better how to make this happen.

MAY 9

Still not pregnant.

The doctor has given Sam some vitamins to take and suggested some other things we can do to increase our chances of me getting pregnant.

It's best for me to never talk about any of this with Sam. He feels bad enough about it as it is.

Sometimes for us now being intimate is like conducting a medical procedure.

We don't talk much about having kids anymore. It's too painful.

Sometimes after he's asleep, I get up and go in the living room and have myself a good cry.

I just want to be a mom.

MAY 21

Sam graduated today! His whole family was here for the graduation. My mom and dad sent a card and a check but didn't come because they were vacationing back in their old neighborhood in New Jersey.

Last night I baked him a cake for the occasion. Apparently you're supposed to wait for the cake to cool before you put on the frosting so after I ripped off the top of the cake trying to put the frosting on, I mixed the whole thing up and called it Graduation

Pudding Delight. I told him it was an old family tradition passed down from generation to generation. He either bought it or had the good sense to keep his mouth shut.

Sam's got himself a job in Rapid City, South Dakota, which apparently is a great place to live because of the Black Hills, but mainly because we'll be there together.

SUNDAY, MAY 30

We went to our new ward today in Rapid City. Great people, very friendly.

We got there a little late and sat in the back. I noticed a few Indians around where we were sitting. Most of the Indian men didn't wear white shirts or ties.

After sacrament meeting only a few Anglo members came back and talked to them. Some of the Indians left after sacrament meeting.

For us though it was a friendly ward. We loved staying after church and talking.

We're renting a three bedroom house. We don't have enough furniture to fill the rooms so we use packing boxes as end tables.

At home. after we ate, I went into our bedroom and grabbed a blanket from the closet, wrapped it around me and went in to Sam, sitting in our lonely couch in the living room. One couch, one lamp, and that's it.

"Sammy, Boy, you are now an official member of my tribe."

He got that grin I knew so well. "Does this, by any chance, involve me being allowed to spend the night in your teepee?"

I gave him my most alluring smile. "Maybe so, if you play your cards right." I plopped down next to him. He reached out to pull me in closer. "But first a message from our sponsor. I'm thinking we should start going to church late and sit in the back, with you not wearing a white shirt and tie. I'm hoping we can be friends with the American Indians at church."

"How come? We haven't been called to do that."

"No, but we've been called to be like Jesus. That's all the calling we need."

"That's not the way things are done in the church."

"Work with me here, Pale Face. Let's try it next Sunday and see how it works. Okay?"

"Okay."

"I'm done talking."

We looked at each other with big smiles on our face.

The rest is history.

It's a relief to have left our young married ward at BYU because we don't get an update every Sunday about who else just got pregnant.

We've decided to just enjoy what we have.

SUNDAY JUNE 6

"I can't do this," Sam said as we got ready for church.

"Sure you can."

Sam was complaining about me insisting we go to church late and he not wear a white shirt and tie.

"Why can't I wear a white shirt?" he asked, looking in his closet.

"It's only one Sunday. How about this?" It was a plaid hunting shirt.

"No way."

"Okay, let's go with the checkered shirt with no tie. That's a start."

We arrived late, just before the sacrament hymn began. We looked for some Indian members of the church to sit near. There was a grandmother and her two grand-kids and an older man sitting alone. We sat down in front of the grandmother and the kids.

After sitting down, I turned around and introduced ourselves.

The grandmother smiled but didn't say anything.

After the sacrament, Sam leaned over to me. "The bishop is staring at us."

"So, stare back."

There were many great testimonies given that day.

I picked up my drawing pad and drew an elephant on roller skates.

One of the kids behind us started giggling.

I turned around and smiled and gave her the picture.

A few minutes later the two grandchildren, both girls, were sitting next to me, which meant Sam had to move over one seat.

I drew them both on Indian ponies riding across the plains.

"You draw good," the older girl, maybe nine, said.

"Thanks. What's your name?"

"Cecilia, and this is my sister Mary."

"My name is Charly and this is my husband Sam."

Sam leaned over and said softly. "We're not supposed to be talking now. We're bothering people."

"We're sitting in the back. There's hardly any other people back here so that means we're not bothering anyone."

"The bishop is still staring at us," he said.

By the end of the meeting, Mary was sitting on my lap. I drew a picture of the Savior in the New World after his resurrection teaching the people. And I drew Cecilia and Mary there with the other children, near the Savior.

Pretty soon we were joined by two other Indian kids. Sam was now even farther from me.

After the closing prayer, Sam and I went around introducing ourselves to everyone in the over flow area.

Delphine, Cecilia and Mary's grandmother, said that they needed to go.

"No, stay. Cecilia and Mary should go to Primary," I said.

"It's better for us not to stay," Delphine said softly.

"It is?" I asked.

"Yes."

"Okay then, well, thanks for coming. Come next Sunday and we'll be here."

They left.

The bishop had started to come our way to talk to us but had been stopped by somebody on his way, so he didn't make it to us until after Delphine and her grandkids had left.

He asked if he could talk with us in his office.

We went to his office. After some get-acquainted talk, he cleared his throat and looked at Sam. "What priesthood do you hold?"

"I'm an elder."

"Have you served a mission?"

"Yes."

"I noticed that you weren't wearing a white shirt and tie today. That seems strange to me for someone who's served a mission. Would you mind telling me why you came dressed like that?"

He glanced at me. "My wife thought that if we were dressed more like the Indian members and sat with them, we'd be able to make friends easier."

"Is that also why you came late?" he asked.

"Yes, that was Charly's idea too. Normally I'm on time to my meetings."

He nodded.. "I need to say something to you both."

"Okay," Sam said, no doubt thinking he was going to tell us to shape up.

He paused. "You two are an answer to a prayer I offered this morning."

He then called us to teach primary to the American Indian kids from age five to eleven. Big age spread, right? He's hoping that at some point they'll feel comfortable being in a class with Anglos their age.

Sam asked the bishop if he could wear a white shirt and tie. The bishop said he should consult with me on that.

I kidded with him all the way home how I thought he should dress like a cowboy. He just smiled faintly like he used to do before I came into his life.

"Sammy, don't you know how great this is? It means God trusts us with these kids. There's nothing better than that."

The moment I said it I hoped so much that Sam wouldn't turn to me and ask why, if God trusted us with these kids, why doesn't he trust us with some of our own? If he'd said that, I would have been devastated.

But he didn't say it. Maybe he didn't even think it. But I did. I think about it all the time.

SUNDAY, SEPTEMBER 12

I really need to do better about writing in here more often. My goal now is to write every Sunday after church

Sam and I are so happy teaching Primary to these kids. And Sam, my strait-laced hubby, has become Puppet Master, using hilarious voices for various characters he comes up with to teach part of the lesson. He cracks me up so much that the kids look at me reacting to him and they start laughing too.

These kids are so much more at ease with us now. Now when they first walk into the overflow area (where we always sit) for sacrament meeting, some of them come over for a big hug from me and sometimes even Sam.

There are more Indian families at church now than before we started teaching primary.

We love them so much!

SEPTEMBER 16

Sam and I have been asked to home teach the families of four of our Lakota kids. We visited them tonight. At some of the homes when the kids realized it was us, they came running out of the house and gave me big hugs.

SEPTEMBER 24

Sam is worried because I've recently bought some Indian medallions and jewelry from the moms of these kids. When they need money for gas to go back to the res, they bring something to our home and ask if I'd like to buy it. They know I always will. I've sent about ten things to my family...more than they want or can use for sure.

I know Sam doesn't think that's right, but I tell him it's from money I'll be receiving from my kids' book, so it's not impacting our own budget.

SUNDAY, OCTOBER 3

I'm pregnant! Found out this week officially from my doctor, but had tested it before then at home.

I'm going to have a kid! We'll name our baby either Katie or Adam after the two kids on the plane that changed my whole outlook on how great it would be to be a mom.

I wish I could contact them and tell them what an effect they have had on my life, but I'm not even sure how one would begin to do that.

Sam is walking with a certain swagger. It's so funny to see, and I haven't pointed it out to him, because he would deny the whole thing. But it's there. Yes, sir, no doubt about it, my hubby is a virile man! Oh, yeah!

Seriously, do guys ever grow up? I haven't seen any evidence they do. But it's okay because I love my guy so much.

Oh, one thing. I haven't told him about my choice of names for our first kid. I hope he'll go along with my choice, Katie or Adam.

SUNDAY, OCTOBER 30

164

I was too sick today to go to church. I told Sam he'd have to teach by himself. He called me after sacrament meeting. He said Delphine had told him that she couldn't have him teaching her grandkids without me in the room. I asked why and he says some man had done some bad things to Cecilia so now she's afraid of being in a room with a man.

"But we've got about ten kids in our class now. So what's the problem?" I ask Sam.

He says, I'm only telling you what she told me. Can you come and just sit in the classroom? (He'd walked to church in case I needed the car, which I told him I wouldn't. But he left it anyway.)

I look so awful, I go.

Please, Charly.

Okay. I'll meet you in our classroom after sharing time.

I threw on some clothes and drove to the church. I parked and hurried into the church. I passed two ward members talking in the hall but I didn't say anything to them and they were too shocked to say anything to me.

A few minutes later Sam and the kids in our class came in. Sam must have told them about me because they didn't ask me why I looked so awful. They just nodded and sat down.

"What's the matter with you?" Cecilia asked.

"Morning sickness. I'm pregnant."

She nodded and smiled and said she'd be right back.

A few minutes later she returned with Delphine.

Delphine sat next to me. She had a small branch of a tree maybe four inches long. She broke off about a half-inch section and handed it to me. "Put this in your mouth."

I did.

"If you need more, let me know." And then she left.

Once Delphine left, I went to take the twig out of my mouth.

"Leave it in," Cecilia said.

So I left it in.

About fifteen minutes later I didn't feel sick anymore.

I lasted through Sam's lesson, then told him I'd be in the car. I didn't want anyone seeing me dressed the way I was.

Before I left, I hugged Cecilia and told her to thank her grandmother for me.

I've been much better all day.

NOVEMBER 8

My mom called to ask how I was doing. I told her I was doing very well and that I had something that really helped. She asked me what it was. I couldn't tell her I was chewing on random tree branches, so I just told her it was organic.

NOVEMBER 20

I was running out of the twig so we went over to Delphine and asked for more. She led us in her back yard and cut off a foot long branch from her tree and gave it to me.

Sam started asking her questions about what kind of a tree this was. She shook her head. "You have your ways, we have our ways. I'm doing this because you are my friends and you are helping Cecilia and Mary. I hear them singing songs now they learned in Primary. Thank you."

I gave her a big hug when we left.

DECEMBER 8

Fast Sunday. Of course I didn't fast but I did go to church and bore my testimony. Mostly about Jesus Christ and the atonement and how grateful I am for Him taking upon Him our sins.

After church Sam had meetings. It's okay though. When he comes home, I'm glad he's been tutored in how to be a priesthood man from our bishop and others. I think it's helping him care more about others.

I talked to my mom after church. She asked if we'd be coming home for Christmas.

I said I didn't know but I'd talk with Sam and get back to her.

I'm feeling better these days, even without the magic twigs that Delphine keeps us stocked with.

DECEMBER 21

We started today on our way to SLC for Christmas. We got in a blizzard near Rock Springs so it was slow going. But we made it.

JANUARY 3

What a relief to be back in our place in Rapid City.

When Sam and I got married, I thought it would be great that both sets of our parents lived there. That way we would need to make only one trip to see them. The one thing I hadn't anticipated is how both sets of parents want us to be with them all the time.

Christmas was on a Saturday. Because Sam's brothers and sisters were there for Christmas, we stayed the night with everyone Christmas Eve. Their kids got us up early and we opened presents and then had a big breakfast.

After lunch we went over to my mom and dad's (and Granny) place. We opened presents with them and stayed for dinner.

It was okay, mostly, except for Dad making subtle criticisms of the Church as it relates to state and local government.

Sam handled it well. He just said, "We've been gone so long out of Utah we're not really up on local issues."

"I suppose our grand-kids are going to be raised to be Mormons too, is that right?" my dad asked.

"That's right, Dad. Isn't that great? We hope they serve missions too."

"Big waste of time and money if you ask me."

Granny to the rescue. "Actually, I don't remember anyone asking your opinion on that subject," she said.

That made him mad. He picked up his plate and went into his den to watch football.

"What do we do now?" I asked my mom.

"We stay here and have a nice time," she said.

And so we did.

On our way out Sam and I stopped in and said goodnight to my dad. He didn't even turn down the sound. But he did wave half-heartedly so I guess that's good.

The next day I went snowboarding with Sam's family. Because I'm pregnant, I just watched. But Sam had a great time. And it gave me time to talk to Sam's mom about being the mother of a new-born. Which is coming! I can hardly wait!

The next morning Granny called and told me that Mom and Dad were feeling ignored because we were spending all our time with Sam and his family.

"Did they ask you to call me?" I asked.

"No, I just got tired of hearing them complain. I tried to tell them that when you both are in their home, they hear nothing but criticism, so it's no wonder to me why you're staying away."

"What did they say?" I asked.

"They accused me of being on your side. But hey, there's nothing new about that. I've always been on your side."

"We'll come visit them soon," Sam said.

It went okay I guess. At least my mom appreciated us coming.

We stayed the night at my folks' place. Because of their move to Utah, it wasn't the same bedroom I'd had growing up but it was the same bed and the same furniture and the same paintings on the wall that I'd studied even as a child, fascinated that someone could make a whole new world for people like me to experience.

I tried to let Sam understand what it was like for me growing up in that setting, surrounded by art work I loved. We were in bed and I turned on the lights and tried to tell him what it was like for me and what each painting came to mean to me.

I thought he'd be interested, but once I get him in bed, he's got a one-track mind. Excuse me, a two-track mind. The other track is sleep. That night he was on the sleep track. Too bad, Sam. I could have let you understand how my artistic mind works.

NEXT DAY

I think we were both glad when we could say goodbye and head back to South Dakota.

MARCH 19

Sam came home today worried he might lose his job. Business is way down. I tried to be upbeat. "So, if you do, you'll find something else."

But, truth is, I am worried. But there's nothing I can do about it so I'll just keep on my happy face.

APRIL 4

We watched conference this weekend. It was good not to have to get dressed for church.

I am so huge! My maternity clothes are now almost too small. From the front I look okay but from the side I look like a short torpedo.

It won't be long now! I can hardly wait! JUNE 12, MY BABY ADAM'S BIRTH DAY!!

(Added two weeks later) When Adam was born, he was 6 pounds five ounces and 21 inches tall.   Brown hair but not much of it. Blue eyes but that might change.

When I was in labor, there was another expectant mom in there with me. Sally Wilson.

I had Sam with me but Sally didn't have anyone. I asked her about it and she said her husband was a rodeo cowboy and he was at a rodeo in Denver and wouldn't be back for three days. I asked if she had anyone to help her when she got home and

174

she said not really but she was sure she could handle it.

"We should invite Sally and her baby to stay with us after our babies are born," I said to Sam.

"Yeah, right," he said, thinking I couldn't be serious.

I had Sam give me a priesthood blessing. It really helped. I asked Sally if she'd like one too. She said she would. So Sam gave her a blessing too.

A short time later, Sally and I seemed to be having a race to see who could deliver first.

The next time the nurse came in and checked me out, she said, "You're good to go, Gal. Let's get you into the delivery room."

They had Sam put on a gown so he could go in and watch.

Another hour of not much happening except pain and we got to this point where the nurse says, "One more push."

I winced and gritted my teeth and pushed as hard as I could.

And out came Adam, my baby boy, my son!

They took him away to clean him up and returned me back to the first room I'd been in.

A few minutes later they brought my son back and put him in my arms.

My son. My Adam. My baby. I was so happy. I cried tears of joy.

"We got ourselves a baby, Sam."

"Looks that way."

"Say hello to your son."

"Hello, this is your father speaking."

"How warm, how affectionate," I teased.

Sally was next. They brought her back a while later.

"How'd it go?" I called out.

"Okay I guess. I got me a boy."

"What are you going to call him?"

"Tex Wilson."

"This is South Dakota," Sam said.

"I know. My husband is from Texas."

"Is it okay if Sam goes in and sees your baby," I asked.

"Oh, yeah, sure! That'd be great."

I pulled him down and whispered to him. "When you come back in here after seeing her baby, you know what to say, right?"

He nodded. "I do."

"I knew you would."

This is what Sam told me afterwards. When he returned to the viewing area and asked if they could wheel the Wilson baby closer to the viewing window, the nurse looked puzzled and asked, "Weren't you just here for Charlene Roberts's baby?"

"Yeah, so?"

She gave him a weird look and shrugged her shoulders, and left to wheel Sally's baby boy close enough so he could get a good look.

When he returned to Sally and me, he was a little too enthusiastic for me. "What a great looking kid, Sally! Where'd he get all that hair?"

"From his dad.'

"Good job you two!"

I felt like I was going to cry.

He noticed. "Oh, sorry," he said.

"It's okay." I paused. "You do like our baby though, right?"

"I do, very much."

I sighed. "Good. He'll grow hair."

He felt bad. "I know he will, but he's perfect now."

"Sorry, I'm so emotional now."

"It's okay. You were amazing."

I decided he was right. I am amazing and so is my baby!

JUNE 14

I'm home now with Adam along with Sally and her son Tex. My mom can't come for three more days. Poor Sam. Sally and I are keeping him hoping, taking care of two new moms.

He's been so heroic in all this. Fixing us food, going to the store for more diapers and baby powder, holding one of our babies while either Sally or me take a long bath.

JUNE 16

Sally's husband Dwayne came today. He's a tall, lean, quiet cowboy. He took Sally and her baby back home.

When she left, she hugged me and thanked Sam and me for being so good to her.

"Let's keep in touch," I said. "If you two are ever in town, come stay with us."

A couple of hours after Sally left us, Sam picked up my mom at the airport.

I'm so happy she's here to help me through this.

JUNE 22

My mom left today. I'll miss her. Sam maybe not so much. She once mentioned to us how well Mark was doing. Sam didn't appreciate that at all. Me either for that matter.

Poor Sam had to go grocery shopping for us and buy coffee for my mom. It might as well been whiskey in terms of him worrying that some member of our ward would see him with coffee in his cart. But as far as we can tell, he made it without being caught.

I am so tired all the time. I never get enough sleep. I feed my baby and then fall asleep and then have to feed him again. All through the night and all through the day.

The most I do for exercise is take baths but even that tires me out. This is so much harder than I ever thought it would be. How do women do this more than once?

Poor Sam. I know I'm neglecting him but after taking care of my baby I don't have any energy left.

SUNDAY, JULY 4

Today Sam blessed Adam in sacrament meeting. I was blown away by the experience. I felt the spirit. I'm so grateful that Sam lives in such a way as to be receptive to the Spirit. He gave Adam such a wonderful blessing. I'm so grateful for my membership in the church.

Later I bore my testimony. And, yes, I used those stupid tissues they keep up there. I'm becoming so predictable.

My only regret is that my mom and dad and Granny weren't there...not just there but I'm sorry they don't believe the same things I now believe.

SATURDAY, JULY 17

Sam and I ventured out and went shopping in a shopping mall just because I needed to get out of the house. We left Adam with a fifteen year old girl from our ward. We promised to be back within an hour. We left right after I'd nursed him. And we left him sleeping.

As we were walking around the mall, I saw a young mom standing off to the side holding her baby. She seemed to be studying shoppers as they walked past.

After we passed her, I stopped.

"What's wrong?" Sam asked.

"That woman needs help."

"How do you know that?"

"The way she looks at the people walking by."

"But she's just standing there. She's not even asking for a handout."

"Let's go talk to her," I said.

"They have agencies that help needy people you know."

"I'm going over to talk to her. Are you coming with me or not?" I said.

He sighed, shrugged and we headed over to the woman.

She was about my height with long brown hair. It looked like we might be about the same age too. Her clothes were plain and there was a button missing from the shirt she was wearing.

"Hi there," I said to her. "How old is your baby?" I asked

"Four months."

"She's beautiful."

She smiled. "Thank you."

"So, what brings you shopping today?" I asked.

She lowered her gaze.

"You can tell us," I said.

"I don't have any food."

"How come?"

"My husband is working in Alaska. He didn't send me any money this week...or last week either."

"So why did you come here?" Sam asked. "I mean, there are places where you can go if you need a handout, right?"

"I was hoping I'd see someone I knew from where we used to live that I could ask."

"Where'd you used to live?" I asked.

"Gillette, Wyoming."

"That's kind of a long shot," Sam said.

She nodded. "I didn't know what else to do. I don't know anyone here."

"Sometimes churches help out people like you," Sam said.

I wondered how Sam could be so clueless.

"Or the government," he continued.

I stared at Sam. "Are you done?"

"I'm just saying…"

I turned to the mom. "How much do you need?"

"Ten or fifteen dollars."

I turned to Sam. "She needs fifteen dollars."

He sighed and pulled two tens out of his wallet. "Do you have change?" he asked.

I sighed. "Sam, just give her all of it."

He handed her twenty dollars.

She lowered her head. "Thank you."

"Yeah, sure," Sam said. He turned to me. "Let's go."

I turned to the woman. "What's your name?"

"Laura."

"That's a beautiful name. And what is the name of your baby?"

"Monica."

"Beautiful name, beautiful baby. You must be very proud of her."

"I am."

"We have a baby too. It's a boy and his name is Adam."

She nodded. "I wish I could see him."

"Me too. We love to show him off as I'm sure you do with Monica. Let me ask you a question. What will you do if your husband doesn't send you any money this week too?"

"I'll call my dad and ask him to come get me. I'm from a little farm town in Illinois, about eighty miles from Chicago. My dad has never liked my husband and told me that someday he'd abandon me." She sighed. "Maybe he was right. I'll give it another week and then call my dad."

"Okay, well let us know if there's anything we can do. Here, let me give you our number."

"That's not a good idea," Sam said to me privately.

I shook it off and gave Laura our phone number.

As we were leaving, she touched me on the shoulder. I turned to face her.

"God sent you to me," she said softly.

I nodded. "I know."

We walked away. "Well, I'll say one thing. She's good at what she does," Sam said cynically.

"What are you talking about?"

"The whole 'My baby doesn't have any food' bit. That's quite effective. I wonder how much she pulls in a week with that line. I'd bet it's at least five hundred, maybe more."

"She was telling the truth," I said.

"Oh, really? And how, may I ask, do you know that?"

"From her eyes."

"If we follow her, she'll go someplace else and do the same bit again. That's what these people do."

"No, she'll go to a store and buy some food and then go to where she's living and then she'll feed herself and her baby."

"You want to make a bet on that?" Sam asked.

"No, I don't."

We continued shopping.

Half an hour later we were in our car on our way back to our place and we saw Laura walking with a bag of groceries and her baby in her arms.

"Let's stop and give her a ride," I said.

Sam stopped. I got out of the car. "Can we give you a ride back to your place?"

She smiled. "Yes, thank you."

She got in the car. "I'm glad I saw you. If you give me your address, I will send back the money you loaned me when my husband sends me money this week."

I wrote down our name and address and gave it to her.

We dropped her off at an apartment building where she lived. Sam offered to carry in her groceries. She said that would be a big help. So he did.

On the way home Sam didn't say anything so I didn't know what he was thinking.

We pulled into our driveway but Sam didn't get out. "She had baby formula, some baby food, and Raman Noodles in her bag," he said quietly.

"Okay."

He shook his head. "So I was wrong about her."

I shrugged. "No big deal."

"No, it is. What is wrong with me? I was raised in the Church my whole life. I've studied the Sermon on the Mount a lot of times. I graduated from seminary. I served a mission. I took religion classes at BYU. And what has all that taught me? Apparently nothing."

He continued. "In the parable of the Good Samaritan, I'm the priest who sees a need and walks by. When I see someone in trouble, these are the things I think. In Utah, I think, 'I hope this guy's home teachers or bishop know about this so they can help.' Or I think, 'If this guy was living the gospel, he wouldn't be in this fix.' Or here in Rapid City I think, 'I hope county welfare knows about this guy.' That's it. That's all I got. I'm not like you. I've never been like you. But now for the first time I wish I was more like you. I wish I were better at following the teachings of Jesus Christ. The only time I help anyone is when my elders quorum president calls me up and asks."

"You helped me become a member of the Church. I will always be grateful to you for that," I said.

"I know but what good is the priesthood if I don't care about others?"

"You do care about others. I feel so loved and appreciated by you. And you know how Adam's eyes light up when you come into the room. And your mom and dad know how much you love them. And your sisters and their kids.."

"The Good Samaritan was not related to the man who'd been robbed and beaten. I'd have walked past him too, like the others did."

"I don't think so."

"No, I would. I used to think that I was going to be a good example for you. But it's just the opposite. You're my example. Thank you for not giving up on me."

"Truth is, Bucko, we're a good team. That's all God needs."

"Thank you for taking a chance on me and agreeing to marry me."

"It is an honor to be married to you, Sam. And I mean that."

"I'll try to get better at the Good Samaritan thing."

"Good, because I could use some help today from you."

"At your service, Ma'am. Your wish is my command."

"We need to mop the floor in the kitchen and vacuum the carpet."

He nodded. "What would you like me to start with?"

"I'll feed Adam and you start vacuuming."

And that's what we did. I appreciated his help so much.

JULY 26

At work today they told Sam they were going to have to let him go. They're giving him two week's pay but told him he didn't need to show up anymore.

He called his dad who said he'd see what he could do to find him a job

JULY 29

Sam's dad called and said he'd found two possible jobs for him.

We're leaving tomorrow, pulling a U-Haul trailer with all our belongings, which didn't even fill the trailer.

AUGUST 15

We're back in SLC. And Sam has a job. We're renting a house with the option to buy. It's a tiny house but all we need right now.

It's so great to bring Adam to Sam's folks or mine and leave him there so we can have a small break from being parents.

My dad is particularly good with Adam. He gets down on the floor and holds him up so it looks like he's walking. And he talks to him in a funny voice. I suppose he must have done that with me.

At first I resented it because he and I haven't been close since Mom found out he was having an affair with his secretary.

This makes me realize how wide the gap still is between us now. I wish I could just forget his past mistakes but I seem stuck where I am.

One night I asked Sam, "What would cause you to leave me for another woman?"

"Nothing in the world would cause me to do that."

"What if she's drop-dead gorgeous?"

"Charly, we've made covenants in the temple before God that we will be faithful to each other forever. I keep my covenants with God. End of story."

I guess he could see that even though he'd given a good answer it wasn't totally working for me. So he threw this in, "And, of course, I love you with all my heart and soul."

That was a little better. I nodded. "Okay. Thanks. Please hug me."

He did.

SATURDAY, OCTOBER 2 (CONFERENCE)

It's been a long time since I've written here. I've been so busy with Adam that by the end of the day I'm so tired I just want to get some sleep.

Two of the talks today (Saturday) were on how we should forgive others. It seemed like they were talking directly to me. I know I need to go talk with my dad and try to make things better between him and me.

The only trouble is that I'm not sure how to do that.

SUNDAY

Between sessions of conference, I went over to talk to my dad. He was watching football on TV.

"Dad, can we talk?"

He glanced at me. "What about?"

"About us."

He paused. "Can this wait four more minutes? The game will be over then."

"Sure, no problem."

Four minutes on the clock in an NFL game means fifteen to twenty minutes.

I sat down on an old dining room chair off to the side and not next to him on the couch.

In the last few seconds of the game, the team that had been losing made a field goal and tied up the game, which meant they had to keep playing.

"Some game, huh?" my dad said.

"Yeah, for sure," I said, thinking maybe I should just leave and forget the whole thing.

Another five minutes, though, and then finally, mercifully, it was over.

The phone rang. My dad answered. It was an old friend from high school. They talked about the game for several more minutes.

And then my dad said he had to go. With that over, he turned to me. "What's up?"

"One of the conference talks today was on forgiving others. I realized I've never forgiven you for...uh... the affair you had with your secretary. And so I was hoping we could talk about it so I can work on trying to forgive you and, hopefully, we can move on."

"I didn't have an affair with my secretary."

"Oh, c'mon, I know better than that. It was when I was in ninth grade."

"Ninth grade? And you're just bringing this up now?"

"Don't you think somebody should have told me what was going on?"

"What was I supposed to say? How could you possibly understand what was going on?"

"What's there to understand? You left us for another woman."

"That is simply not true."

"Mom would go in her room and close the door and turn on the radio so I wouldn't hear it and then she'd cry. At first she wouldn't answer me when I asked where you were. And then she said you were on a business trip. And when I asked when you'd be back, she said she didn't know. And when you finally did come back, she made you promise to either fire your secretary or get her assigned to another office. I could hear you two talking about it."

"So you think that while I was gone, I was with Madge? That's not true. Your mom threw me out of the house and I rented a place until she'd let me come back. I never lived with Madge."

"What did you do that made Mom so mad she threw you out of the house?"

"Okay, once at a Christmas office party, Madge and I both had too much to drink and we ended up in a supply room kissing. Somebody saw us and, well, that got back to your mom and she threw me out. So all it was, really, was a few kisses in a supply room after we'd both had too many drinks. It certainly was not a full-blown affair."

"You're saying Mom over-reacted?" I shot back.

"No. I'm not saying that. You're right. I betrayed the trust she had in me. And that was wrong. But have you ever wondered why this happened in the first place? I bet you haven't. You just want to put all the blame on me. But that's never the case."

"I don't want to hear you complain about Mom!" I stormed out of the house.

Two days later my dad came over and asked if we could take a walk. After about a block, he said, "This happened during a time when your mother and I were having problems. But that was no excuse for what I did. But even though it was very wrong, it wasn't adultery. I'd just had too much to drink is all. It was just a few kisses in a backroom where we worked. I had Madge transferred to another office...with no drop in pay I might add."

I shrugged. "I assume that was so you wouldn't have a law suit on your hands."

He shrugged. "I can't say that didn't have some part in me treating her fairly."

"Did you apologize to Mom?" I asked.

"I did, but more than that I've never given her a reason to wonder about my loyalties to her after that."

"Good. So there's just me. You never talked to me."

"I didn't know you knew anything about this."

"I knew that Mom threw you out. I knew that you were gone a few weeks. I knew that during that time she spent a lot of time in her bedroom crying. I knew that when you did come back, you two could hardly stand to be in the same room with each other. And I knew that somehow it involved your secretary."

"Is that why you spend as little time with me as possible? Why you glare at me whenever I'm with Adam? Why you won't let me take him with me sometimes?"

"Yes, that's why."

"Okay, this is much too late, but I apologize to you for the effect what I did had on you. Now let's just move on, okay? It's water under the bridge as they say."

That was it. He was done. It wasn't all that I wanted but it was better than nothing. And I probably wasn't going to get more than that from him.

I told him I accepted his apology. I also apologized for not bringing it up sooner and for having bad feelings about him ever since then.

He cleared his throat and suggested we turn around and head back.

As we started up the sidewalk to Sam's folks' house, as a token of trust, I said, "If you want to come sometime and take Adam in his stroller for a walk, that would be good."

He smiled. "Thank you. I would very much like to do that."

So we're okay I guess. Except a part of me is still mad at him. I can say I forgive him but I'm not sure if I'll ever be able to completely forgive him. Either he doesn't know that or he doesn't care.

One thing I know. I don't want to think about this anymore.

OCTOBER 13

I took Adam over to spend some time with my folks and Granny. In the past few days my dad has spent a fortune. They have more toys in their house than we do.

Granny showed me a painting she was working on. It's totally amazing! She asked me if I was working on anything.

"I'm about to start on something," I told her. "The people who commissioned have been very patient but I will need to get going on it soon."

"What's it going to be?"

"The shortest passage of scripture in the Bible. 'Jesus wept.'"

"Interesting. I can hardly wait to see what you do with that theme."

On our way down the stairs, she stopped. "I was wondering if you and Sam would be willing to go with me to some symphony concerts once in a while and, also, an occasional exhibit at the art museum."

"Yeah, sure, we'd love to do that."

"Good because I've just made the three of us patrons of the arts for the Utah Symphony and also for the art museums in town. We get free tickets and an occasional reception." She handed me two wallet size cards.

"The next Utah Symphony concert is in a couple of weeks or so," she said. "Talk to Sam about coming with us. Oh, I'll throw in dinner too as an added benefit."

She's so great!

OCTOBER 14

Adam is such a delight to Sam and me. Every day is like a gift to us as he gains new skills. Like his smile. His smile reminds me of his dad, which makes it even more endearing.

NOVEMBER 4

Last night we dropped off Adam with my folks and grabbed Granny for our big night out attending the Utah Symphony concert.

We had a great time! Or at least Granny and I did. Sam said he did but I noticed that after each piece the orchestra performed, Sam put a big check mark next to it on the program like he was thinking. "Okay, that one's over. Only four more to go." But maybe I was reading too much into that.

However he did seem disappointed when they did an encore.

When we picked up Adam, he was asleep so we carefully got him ready for bed and laid him down.

And he kept sleeping! Yes!

For Sam (and me too I guess) this was play time. "Do you happen to know that I am a big supporter of the arts in this town?" Sam asked.

"You are?" I said, trying to sound as naïve as possible.

"Oh, yes. The arts are my life, really."

"I am so impressed with that!"

"The arts are very important to me so I like to support them. financially. In fact I have my membership card right here for the Utah Symphony Supporters if you'd like to see it." He proudly showed me the card.

"That is so cool!" I replied. "I also love and appreciate the arts!"

He leaned into me. "So, in a way, I guess you could say we are in simpatico as they say in Italy. Yes?"

"I guess we are."

He should have left it alone but he didn't. "I support actual art too, you know, like actual paintings and, you know, artsy stuff like that."

"That is so good to hear because I am an artist!"

"I could tell."

"How could you tell?"

"The way you have your face painted up. It's very artsy."

It was hard to keep a straight face. "Would you say it's surreal?"

"Oh, yeah, your face is so real!"

I tried not to laugh. "Thank you. You know what? I'm starting to think that you're someone I could totally trust."

He moved in. "Oh, yes! I am for certain that person! Would you mind if I kissed you? Seeing how we both support the arts in this community."

"I guess that might be okay."

We kissed and then dropped the role playing and hurried to get ready for bed.

Overall, it was a great night. My only worry is that Sam's going to be using the "I support the arts in this community" from now on whenever he's in the mood for love.

But it's okay. He's fun to be with. And he makes me laugh.

It's almost surreal.

SUNDAY, NOVEMBER 28

This past week I started on a commissioned piece based on the quote from Matthew, "Jesus wept."

TUESDAY

I'm so proud of Sam today.

Our next door neighbor, Brother Latimer, is a widower in his seventies. He always takes great care of his property and is usually the first one in the neighborhood shoveling his driveway and sidewalk after it snows.

Last night it snowed six inches. Sam did our walk and driveway and then noticed that that Brother Latimer wasn't out shoveling as usual. So he went to his house and knocked on the door. Brother Latimer called out for whoever was at the door to come in.

Sam went in and found Brother Latimer lying on his couch. He told Sam he'd slipped and fell when he was in his backyard trying to shovel his patio. Sam asked if he needed to go see a doctor. Brother Latimer said no but that he'd appreciate if Sam could make him some oatmeal and pour him some orange juice and bring it to him. Oh, also, he wanted his newspaper.

Sam got him all that, asked him if there was anything else he could do.

Brother Latimer said he was worried about his driveway and sidewalk.

Sam said, "I can do that for you."

Brother Latimer paused and then said that he would very much appreciate that.

So Sam, my man, went to work. It took him about half an hour.

Why am I so proud of him for that? Because he didn't think, "Maybe I should call the elders quorum president and find out who Brother Latimer's home teachers are. And then the elders quorum president will call and ask them to shovel him out."

Sam has such a ordered mind that's the way his mind works. But I'm fairly certain that's not what Jesus was trying to teach with the parable of the Good Samaritan. I think He was saying, "If you see a need, try to fill it." And that's what Sam did today! I am so proud of him for that!

I love this man!

After Sam left for work, I realized the ball was now in my court. I called Sam's mom and said, "Okay, I never thought I'd say this, but can you teach me how to make a casserole?"

"You've made casseroles before, haven't you?"

"Yeah, once. Sam only had one bite and then made himself a peanut butter sandwich. I'm talking about a casserole that people would actually like. Our neighbor hurt his back so I want to bring him a Mormon casserole. You know, like the one you people serve when someone's died."

"You mean funeral potatoes?"

"Yeah, or something like that.

"Come over and I'll show you how it's done."

We had a good time working together.

We made two. One for Brother Latimer and one for us.

As Sam and I cleaned up after dinner, I told him again how proud of him I was for helping Brother Latimer

He smiled. "So if you keep coaching me, there might be hope for me after all," he said.

"Definitely."

CHRISTMAS DAY

A great day for us, made even better because of Adam's reaction to his toys.

Adam has a new game. It's Peek-a-boo. Sam loves to play it with him. Adam laughs with delight!

What a great thing it is to have this wonderful son of ours.

NEW YEAR'S DAY

Things are going good for us. Adam is strong and healthy and growing up so fast.

Sam and I are doing good. I've never been happier in my life than I am right now.

Sam makes me laugh when he plays with Adam.

I'm so lucky to be married to Sam. He's kind and decent and he takes good care of me and he's a great dad and he makes sure we have family prayer and family home evening and he gives us priesthood blessings and he's someone I can go to talk with when I'm having a bad day. I love him so much!

He has a fun side too now and can make me laugh. Like Saturday at ten in the morning when I was sleeping in and he woke me up with a puppet-- him lying on the floor and the puppet my level talking to me, with Adam on the floor next to him.

"Excuse me, Ma'am, but the lad here and me are hankering something fierce for pancakes and bacon, and so, uh, we actually mixed up the batter and fried the bacon, but we were just wondering if you'd care to join us. We'd be mighty honored if you would! And one other thing, where do you keep the maple syrup? Cause it's not in the cupboard."

I rolled over to see the puppet in my face. "What's your name, Little Man?"

"Hank, Ma'am," he said.

"Hank what?"

"Hank E."

"Do people ever blow their noses on you?"

"Them there's fighting words, Ma'am."

I sat up in bed, looked down and saw Sam lying on the floor with a big grin on his face with Adam next to him.

"I've created a monster, haven't I?" I asked.

"Yes, Ma'am, you have."

I got out of bed and gave Sam a quick hug and told him I'd be in the kitchen in a few minutes.

That's what my Sammy has become. Fun to be with! Not up tight and boring when I first met him. I not only love him but I so much enjoy being with him!

I'm starting to think about us having another baby but I haven't mentioned it to Sam yet. Because I'm not sure he's ready to repeat this again.

NEW YEARS'S DAY

Today Sam and I and Adam spent the afternoon with my folks watching football and grazing on snacks.

My dad and I are getting along better now because we talked things over about him and his secretary.

My mom and dad are still complaining that Sam and I and Adam spend more time with Sam's family than with them. But that's because Sam's parents are all the time having family occasions, like baby blessings and anniversaries and birthday parties. And then there's General Conference where we often get together to watch as an extended family.

The only real occasion for my family is when the New York Giants are playing. And then basically you sit in a room and munch non-stop and stand up and yell once in a while.

I'm doing good except for a pain in my back. It's probably from picking up Adam the wrong way and straining my back.

SUNDAY, JANUARY 9

I visit teach Rita Sanchez. She's about my age, married and has two kids. She and her husband are recent converts.

When I first visited her, I asked her why I never saw her at Relief Society. She said she went once but many of the women there were older and she didn't seem to have anything in common with them. Also, Spanish is her first language so it was sometimes hard to understand what people were saying.

So after weeks of inviting her, I finally got her to come to Relief Society with me. Sitting with her and trying to try to imagine what this was like for her, I realized there wasn't much she could relate with.

Sister Jacobs, our teacher for that day, asked what we did with our husbands that brought us closer.

The answers given were: gardening, taking walks together, going to concerts, canning fruit, and going to the temple.

Rita leaned over and whispered another suggestion.

I started laughing. "Good suggestion! Tell them." I said.

She shook her head. "No, I can't say that. You do it."

So I raised my hand and said, "Sam and I like to make love."

Rita laughed so hard. So that was good.

The only trouble was it got back to Sam. I think he was actually okay with it but, even so, he was embarrassed I'd said that in Relief Society.

I can't tell him the real reason I said it (which was to help Rita feel more a part of Relief Society) so I'm just letting him think whatever he wants. Which I imagine is a huge ego boost for him.

Men are so predictable.

SUNDAY, FEBRUARY 6

Rita comes to Relief Society all the time now. I always sit with her but she has other friends too.

She made a big hit with us all when we had a luncheon to celebrate Relief Society's anniversary and she brought guacamole she'd made. It was, as we say, Mucho Grande!

The pain in my back is getting worse. I should probably go see a doctor about it.

FEBRUARY 20

I'm home now but last week I spent three days in the hospital. That pain in my back hit me bad when Sam and I were shopping for groceries. It was so bad I could hardly stand up. Sam took me to ER and they did some tests.

They came back with a shocker.

I have cancer.

It's okay though. Lots of people get cancer and they get treated for it and they live another forty years or so. I'm sure that will be the case with me.

LATER

The doctor talked to Sam and then he came in and we talked. The doctor told me my cancer was not something easily cured with chemo or radiation. Sam wants me to take whatever procedures necessary to get over this. And, really, what other option do we have? I'm not ready to die anytime soon.

FEBRUAY 24

Sam and his dad gave me a priesthood blessing. His dad put the oil on my head and Sam gave the blessing. I felt the spirit part of the time and then not so much. I could feel his dad flinch when Sam promised me a full recovery and a long healthy life.

THE NEXT DAY

While Sam was at work, I called his mom and dad and asked if they could come over and talk.

We talked about the blessing. I told Sam's Dad that I didn't feel Sam had said what God wanted him to say but instead, what he wanted so much. I asked him if he felt that way too. Reluctantly he said he did. I asked him to give me a blessing. The three of us were bawling as he told me that Heavenly Father was aware of what I was going through and that he would help me with his Spirit. And that I needed to have faith in God and know that in the eternal scheme everything would turn out for my family. I felt the spirit confirm what he said even though it's not what I wanted to hear.

He stopped for a little while and then softly he said this in his blessing. "I know you are concerned about your son Adam, if he will remember you after you pass away. I bless you to know that some day he will be very grateful to you and honor you and remember you and the blessing you gave him by giving him life. He will also feel close to you and gain from your example during hard times."

I was sobbing, and he was fighting back tears, Sam's mom was crying too. He paused and then ended his blessing in the name of Jesus Christ.

We agreed we wouldn't tell Sam about this. I don't want him to feel bad that he didn't go by the Spirit but by what he so much wanted.

The bottom line? I'm going to die.

Sam's mom took Adam so I could get some rest, but I didn't rest much. Mainly I cried for what was about to be taken away from me.

MARCH 13

I just figured out the deal about chemo and radiation therapy. It doesn't cure you. It just makes you feel so bad that death seems like a better alternative.

Today I told Sam that I wasn't doing anymore of any chemo or radiation. I wanted to be home all the time to spend as much time as I could with Adam.

That made him mad. He accused me of giving up. It's not giving up when you already know God's will. But I couldn't tell him that. I don't want him to know I asked his dad to give me a blessing after Sam had promised me I'd get better.

MARCH 17

Things are going too fast. It's like I'm behind and I can't catch up. I wake up every morning and start thinking about things I need to do that day. Routine things like shopping for some clothes for Adam. And then reality sets in and it's as much as I can do to get up and get dressed and care for Adam.

In the future someone else will need to buy clothes for Adam.

Not me.

I can't stand this.

I don't want to die!

ABOUT A WEEK LATER

I am ashamed of this now. But I woke up thinking that if I hadn't married Sam, if I'd stayed in NYC with Mark, I'd never have got cancer. That somehow living in Utah had given me cancer. And that maybe if I went back to Mark, then things would return to the way they were.

I thought about phoning Mark. But I didn't. Being with Mark wouldn't change what is going to happen. Besides, didn't my temple wedding mean anything? I started crying. Beating up on myself. Going back to New York won't make me better either. Going back in time isn't possible.

APRIL 8

Today I begged Sam to contact Katie and Adam, the two children I met on the plane on my way to Utah the first time. I wanted him to tell them how much they had blessed my life for helping me see that having kids might not be such a bad thing.

He's trying to find them but I can't give him their last names. I now they had family

in Utah and they lived back East. And that's
about it.

Finally I came to my senses. I told him
he didn't need to keep trying. It wasn't that
important anyway.

APRIL 9

Today I remembered how, when we
were living in Rapid City, Delphine gave me
this twig and it stopped my morning sickness
and so I was thinking that maybe she'd have
something that would cure me of cancer. So I
tried to call her because I didn't want Sam to
have to do that for me too.

I had an old ward list from our ward
in Rapid City so I called the bishop and
asked if he knew where she was. He said he
didn't know but he'd heard she'd moved
back to Rosebud. I tried to find her but I
couldn't. Maybe if Sam and I drove up there,
we could find her and she'd go in her
backyard and pull down a branch of a tree
and tell me to put it in my mouth and I'd be
cured in a couple of weeks.

For a while I was so certain that was the way I was going to get over this. But that feeling lasted only for maybe an hour. I even worked on how we'd get there. We'd fly to Rapid City and then rent a car and then we'd drive to Rosebud and we'd stop at a general store and ask about Delphine and they'd tell us where she lived now and we'd go out there and she'd mix us up something or she'd get hold of a medicine man she knew and he'd mix us something and put it in a canning jar and tell me to get up early in the morning and face the sunrise and take one spoonful and that would cure me in a few days.

So when Sam came home I told him all about it. And he listened and let me say it all, and then he said, "If you want to do that, I'm okay with it. When would you like to leave?"

I was overcome knowing he'd do that for me even though, honestly, it made no sense. It made me break down and bawl because deep in my heart I knew it wouldn't work and that I'm going to die from this and there isn't anything I can do to stop it.

It's too much to take in. I started sobbing. Sam held me in his arms.

When I'd calmed down, he said his mom had made some homemade soup and baked some bread for us and that he'd go get it and bring some for us.

And so we ate our soup and I tried to be upbeat and energetic. Which lasted maybe ten minutes and then I was exhausted and had to rest.

MAY 8

During the day Sam's mom stays with me and Adam. My mom and dad always come but they don't stay as long. I guess because they can see me getting worse every day and that's hard for them.

Granny visits me every day. She stays with me. She makes me feel better. We play cards sometimes. Sometimes she even lets me win.

A FEW DAYS LATER (I can't keep track of what day it is anymore.)

I asked Sam's mom to help me take a bath and fix my hair. So she's doing my hair and talking a mile a minute about little things happening in her family and I look in the mirror and I'm overcome by how much help she is to me all the time. She does our wash. She cooks for us. She comes and takes Adam whenever I'm too sick to watch him. She's like an angel but an angel with a lot of energy. No job is too hard for her.

"I want to go see my mom and dad today," I said to her. "I'll wait for Sam to come home. Can you watch Adam for us?"

"Yes, of course. I'll call Sam and let him know your plans." She paused. "Are you sure it wouldn't be better for them to come over here?"

"No I have to go to them."

Why did I insist on going to see them? Because I wanted to put myself out for them so they'd know how much I love them.

Sam came home early from work and helped me out to the car.

When we pulled into the driveway, Granny came out right away. "Hello, Star Light! We're so happy you came." She called me Star Light when I was little. Or so she told me when I got older. "Star light, Star bright, first star I see tonight."

Sam got the wheelchair from the trunk and wheeled it over to where I can get out of the car and into it.

Once I was in the wheel chair, I touched Granny's hand. "I may need some help."

"Anything. What can I do for you?"

"If I say something stupid, let me know right away so I can apologize."

She nodded. "Okay. But you never say anything stupid."

Even though I wasn't doing much except sitting in my wheel chair, by the time Sam got me into the house I was exhausted.

My mom tried to hide her tears.

We ended up in the living room. "Mom
and Dad, I just wanted to thank you both for
all you've done for me my entire life. I know
I haven't always shown my gratitude but
every day now I look back, and remember
how good you two were to me. I'm sorry I
didn't appreciate what I had when I was
growing up."

I stopped. I felt so weak. Granny came
over and knelt down. "You okay?"

"I'm so tired is all."

"Of course. Do you want to rest for a
while?"

Tears were streaming down my face.
"No, I have to say this. I want them to know
that I love them and I'm sorry for being such
a brat when I was growing up."

She smiled. "I hate to break this to you,
Kid, but the truth is, you're still a brat."

I smiled. Only Granny could get away
with that.

I sighed. "I need to take a nap. And I need my pills. But there's more I want to say to them."

"You can't say it all, and, besides, they already know."

I was sobbing. "I feel so guilty dying on them when I could've been a help to them when they get old."

"I know."

"Granny, I love you so much."

"I love you back, Kid. Always have. Always will."

"There is life after death, Granny."

"You know what? If there is, I want to spend it with you."

"Me too. Can I tell you something? You'll understand this. Sometimes I lie in bed and I think of something I want to paint and I work it all out in my mind, and then I realize I'm running out of time."

She nodded. "That happens to me too. So that can only mean one thing, right?"

"What?"

"There's got to be an art supply store in Heaven, right?"

I smiled through my pain and tears. "Hold my hand, Granny. Help me get through this."

She pulled up a chair and sat down next to me and held my hand.

"Mom, dad, I want you to be close to Adam when he's growing up."

They smiled faintly. "We hope we can do that."

I sighed. There was one unknown that none of us wanted to talk about. And that was how much my mom and dad missed their friends back east. And also, how much contact they had would depend on Sam's second wife. She might think it would confuse Adam. So none of us could know how that was going to turn out.

Mom came over and knelt down and kissed me on the cheek. "I love you so much, Baby."

"I love you too, Mom. Thank you for being such a great mom."

My dad was next. He kissed me on the cheek as well. Tears were rolling down his cheeks. "I love you, Kid."

I smiled up at him. "Too bad I can't take that harp with me when I go. I could probably use it up there."

Granny smiled. "Not in heaven. My guess is that hell can use you though. I can see you tormenting the wretched souls there with your playing."

My dad said. "We'll keep the harp. It will remind us of you."

I nodded.

I felt like I was going to pass out. "I need to go back home right away," I said to Granny.

"Of course," she said, kissing me on the cheek and standing up. She turned to Sam. "Can you get her home now? She's exhausted."

"Yes, of course."

Outside, on our way down the stairs, Sam let the wheel come down on the next stair too hard and it hurt me. "Why don't you watch what you're doing?" I cried out.

"Sorry."

He got me home as quick as he could. I slept most of the rest of the day. But when I woke up, I started crying again and I couldn't stop. Nothing about this seems fair.

THE NEXT DAY

Sam stayed home from work to be with me and Adam. He got me up and into the living room and showed me how Adam could stand up and make his way around by using the couch as a way to keep; from falling. Adam is so delighted he can do this.!

Also, Sam got behind him and supported him so Adam could get the feeling of what it's like to walk. A big smile on Adam.

I was of course delighted to see this but also painfully aware that these first time events will continue long after I'm dead. That thought is very depressing to me.

A FEW DAYS LATER

I felt a little better so when Adam was taking a nap, I called my mom and asked her to come over so we could talk some more.

She came right away. "So, how are you doing, Mom?" I asked.

She seemed surprised by the question. "Isn't that what I'm supposed to ask?"

"I don't know. I think it's best for us both to say everything we can while there's still time. I want to know how you're doing."

"Not too good, actually."

"Can you tell me about it?"

"Sometimes I think that if you hadn't come here, if you hadn't met Sam, then everything would be the way it was, with you in the City."

"With Mark?"

She nodded. "Except married and with two kids."

"Mark with two kids? You do have a rich fantasy life, don't you?"

"I guess so. I'm always trying to make sense out of this. My latest is that there's something in the water here that made you sick or maybe it's the altitude."

"Don't overlook humidity. By the way, did you know that there's a difference in humidity in the East compared with here in Utah?"

She smiled. "I do recall being tutored by Sam on that topic."

"Mister Weather Guy at your service, right?"

"Something like that." She sighed. "I keep trying to make this go away. It doesn't make sense. It's not fair. Let me get sick and die. I've had a good life. Not my baby girl, not my daughter, not our only child. She's supposed to live a long time."

"I know, Mom. I've felt the same way, but I'm resigned to it now. It's been good though, just not long enough."

"I have loved seeing you happily married with a wonderful healthy happy son."

"Me too, Mom."

"I'm just not ready for this other."

"I know. Some days I am, other days I'm a little bitter about the whole thing. Can I tell you something that's helping me? To know that there is life after death and also to know that Sam and I will be married on the other side of the veil. That's a great comfort to me."

"Is that what Mormons believe?"

"Yeah, it is. You and dad should think about having your marriage sealed in the temple for after you're both dead."

"Some days I'm not sure I'd want him after I'm dead."

"I know but who else would you rather have than Dad?"

She smiled. "Let me make a list and I'll get back to you on that."

"You're not fooling me, Mom. You and Dad care for each other."

She shrugged. "Yeah, I suppose you're right."

"You think you'll stay in Utah after I'm gone?" I asked.

"I don't know. Except for our time with you and Adam, we're pretty miserable here most of the time. We miss our friends back in New Jersey. They don't even try to make us change the way we live."

"Yeah, you did have some great friends back home."

"If we do move, we'll come back at least twice a year to be with Adam."

"That would be great. He's going to love being with you because you'll spoil him like crazy."

She smiled. "Yes, we will. Guaranteed."

"Okay, well, as long as he gets to know how much you love him. That's the most important thing."

And then silence.

"Mom, I just want you to know how much I love you and how grateful I am that you were my mom. I know I wasn't easy growing up but you stuck with me and let me know when I was getting off track. I love you so much and I will miss you."

We both started crying. She reached for my hand and held it. I think she was afraid of giving me a hug for fear she'd hurt me.

I could hear Adam waking up. And in a minute he was crying. Mom got up and brought him to me.

"You hold him, Mom."

She did and talked to him in her sweet melodic tones she'd probably used on me when I was Adam's age.

I smiled because it was good to see the love she had for my boy.

A few minutes later Sam's mom returned from grocery shopping.

Mom said she'd better go. She kissed me on the cheek, kissed Adam too and then left.

I'm glad we got to talk.

June 12

Today was Adam's first birthday. We had a small party with just family. Adam had a good time. He liked his presents and the cake.. I tried to be happy and upbeat. That lasted maybe half an hour and then, knowing I was going to cry, I said I was tired and needed to rest. So Sam got me back in bed.

This was my first and last time to celebrate Adam's birthday.

A FEW DAYS LATER

Sometimes Father in Heaven sends a love note. That was the case with me today. Sometimes I have the radio on in my bedroom for when I wake up or when I have to take my pills.

So this afternoon I was asleep and woke up to a preacher reading this: "For I am now ready to be offered, and the time of my departure is at hand. I have fought a good fight, I have finished my course, I have kept the faith: Henceforth, there is laid up for me a crown of righteousness, which the Lord, the righteous judge, shall give me at that day: and not to me only, but unto them also that love his appearing."

This was not a station that I usually listened to. But it was what I needed. But even more than that, it was the influence of the Spirit which told me that this was from Father in Heaven, that He wants me to be at peace with what is going to happen.

I had Sam look it up. It's found in Second Timothy, Chapter 4, verses 6-9.

I cannot deny what I felt. It was real and unmistakable.

I started crying with gratitude that Father in Heaven would do this for me.

I hope I can hang on to the good feeling I will try hard to trust Father in Heaven with my life.

A DAY OR TWO LATER

I wanted Sam to drive me to the Ferris wheel at Liberty Park and then to the SLC temple where we were married. I wanted to tell him how much I loved him and that I would always love him.

But it didn't work out. By the time he got me into the car I was crying so much from the pain that he wheeled me back in and said we'd try it another day.

"I just wanted to tell you how much I love you," I whispered when he put me in our bed.

"I know you love me."

"In the Ferris wheel today I was going to tell you it's been a good ride," I said.

"It has, Charly. A very good ride indeed. I will always love you. Always."

"I know. Me too. I'm so sorry to be bailing out on you."

"I know. Me too."

He kissed me and hugged me and then sat down.

He didn't leave me, watching over me for I don't know how long because I fell asleep.

We have so little time together now.
NEXT DAY

I feel better today so I just wrote up what happened yesterday

There's so much I want to say but I'm running out of time and energy to say it.
A FEW DAYS LATER

Sam brought me breakfast, some toast and some hot chocolate and some pills

"I'm so sorry," I said after I'd had a little to eat.

"Sorry for what?"

"Sorry that I'm going to leave you and Adam alone."

He nodded. And tears came into his eyes. We held hands and both cried.
A FEW DAYS LATER

This was a very bad day. But not because of the pain. I was actually feeling a little better. I had Adam sitting on my lap as we sat by the kitchen table. I drew him a picture of an elephant on a bicycle.

"Can an elephant ride a bicycle?" I asked in the same way I'd talked to Katie on the plane.

No response.

"No, of course not! Here let me try it again." I drew a picture of an elephant as a ballerina.

"Can an elephant be a ballerina?"

Again, nothing from him.

"No, an elephant can't be a ballerina! Mommy's being funny. Mommy's so funny."

I was starting to lose it, knowing my son wouldn't remember any of this. "Adam, please, just once can you say my name? Can you call me Mommy?"

Nothing.

I started crying. "You're not going to even remember me, are you? I'm your mommy and I love you! And you won't even know that. You won't know anything about me! This is so unfair!"

I broke down crying.

A few minutes later Sam's mom came and took Adam and suggested I rest.

And I did. Even though there's so little time for me to be with Adam.

AUGUST 10

I feel better today. I don't know how long it will last so I need to write some things while I can.

Adam, from now on I'm writing in here for you. This started out as a sketch pad and then turned into a diary so you'll read a lot of things that may not make sense to you. But now it's dedicated to you and you alone.

You'll notice little notes to you scattered throughout. They're messages for you.

I've folded back this page. I'll write a note for you to read this page first..

I've just been looking over what became my diary. I have one regret. When I wrote about reading First Nephi, I said that I was glad Nephi had whacked Laban and stole his brass Bible. That was totally inappropriate. Nephi was a prophet of God. He was justified for what he did because Laban had tried to kill him and his brothers at least twice. Also, the Spirit had prompted him to do what he did. And if they hadn't had the brass plates, they would have known nothing about the commandments of God. So please overlook that and know that your mom had a testimony of the truthfulness of the Book of Mormon. I didn't want you to be confused.

Adam, I'm your birth mom. By the time you read this, I'll have been dead for twenty or more years. (Assuming you serve a mission, which I hope you will.)

You don't remember me. I died when you were just a baby. But please know that you've got someone in heaven who's always on your side. Besides Jesus I mean. Oh, and Father in Heaven. And your great grandparents. And maybe even my mom or dad who might also be dead by the time you read this. We've got a real fan club up here dedicated to you. So live with purpose and thoughtfulness because we'll be watching you...if they allow things like that, that is.

I loved you so much when I was alive...and I still love you today.

Oh, one other thing, I don't want to come between you and the mom who's raised you. I just want you to know you have two moms, and I'm one of them. More than anything I wanted to be with you while you grew up but Father in Heaven had other plans for me. I wish I knew why but I don't. So my first lesson is don't ever try to second guess Father in Heaven. Also, I want you to be good to your wife. I wish I'd had a chance to meet her. I'm sure I would have loved her very much.

That reminds me of a story. It's about your dad and me when we lived in South Dakota.

What happened is
Wh
THE NEXT DAY

I'm okay now. In fact, a lot better.

A FEW DAYS LATER

Adam, I need to finish this up.

At first I thought I'd give this to my mom and dad and ask them to save it until you turned twenty, or after your mission, or after your wedding. But now I don't think they're going to stay in Utah after I die, so I talked to Sam's mom and asked if she could save this for you and not let Sam see it because there have been times when I've been critical of him and I don't want him to remember me that way.

So right now your grandparents on your dad's side are coming over and I'm going to give this to them, which means I won't be writing in it anymore.

I'm crying as I write this. I want to say don't forget me. But the truth is you won't remember me at all. So I really can't say that. But this much I can tell you. I won't forget you. Not ever. Not even after I'm dead. I'll be thinking about you all the time.

Do what your dad says. He's a good man. The best I've ever known. I'm so grateful to him for so many things. I will love him forever and I will love you forever.

So I guess we won't see each other until you die, which I hope is not for a long time.

Love Jesus and be good to others.

I love you.

I'm okay.

I'll be okay.

You'll be okay.

We'll all be okay.

Because of Jesus.

Adam, I want you to know that I love Third Nephi beginning with Chapter 11 to the end of the Book of Mormon. Please read it often!

I love Jesus Christ. He is my only hope. I'll see him soon. I hope he gives me a hug and tells me that everything is going to be okay.

They're here. I have to give this up now.

Be good Adam. Please be good.
Everything depends on you being good and
being true and faithful to God.
I love you, Adam!
God be with you until we meet again.
Love,
Mom

ACKNOWLEDGEMENTS
Thanks to Becky Cowley for her two elephant
sketches and also to Natassia Scoresby for a
sketch of Charly in the plane with Adam
and Katie, and also of Charly with two sister
missionaries.

Made in the USA
Monee, IL
07 November 2020